BLOOD KIN

"So you ain't nothing but a whore, just like all the others! My little sister, a stinking, holier-than-thou little—"

Milly slammed her knee up between his legs, and she saw his mouth fly open and felt his hands lose their grip.

In that instant she thought she could escape, and she tore herself free. But somehow he had the strength and luck to deliver a sledgehammer blow to the side of her head.

Milly felt herself slam backward, and then she heard the sound of breaking glass as she crashed through the second-floor hotel window.

As she fell, she also heard her own scream fill her throat and that's the last thing she remembered before she struck the boardwalk . . .

*   *   *

This title includes an exciting excerpt from *Sixkiller* by Giles Tippette, available from Jove Books in May 1992!

Also in THE GUNSMITH series

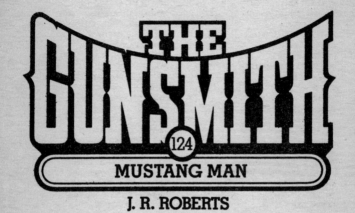

THE GUNSMITH

124

MUSTANG MAN

J. R. ROBERTS

JOVE BOOKS, NEW YORK

MUSTANG MAN

A Jove Book / published by arrangement with
the author

PRINTING HISTORY
Jove edition / April 1992

ISBN: 0-515-10834-0

Jove Books are published by The Berkley Publishing Group,
200 Madison Avenue, New York, New York 10016.
The name "JOVE" and the "J" logo
are trademarks belonging to Jove Publications, Inc.

PRINTED IN THE UNITED STATES OF AMERICA

10 9 8 7 6 5 4 3 2 1

ONE

The West Texas sun was high and hot in July and broiling Clint Adams's brain just as surely as if it were laying in a skillet. The Gunsmith removed his Stetson, squinted into a cloudless sky, and watched a lonely buzzard circle high overhead. The huge bird was gliding on blistering air currents that lifted from the scorched Llano Estacado, and Clint imagined that the buzzard was keeping a hopeful eye on him.

"Not this time," the Gunsmith muttered, yanking down the brim of his hat low over his eyes and taking a drink from his canteen.

Clint raised up in his stirrups and gazed into the heat waves that shimmered to the west. He had been told that there was a little ranching community named Huggins somewhere out in this hellish country, but so far Clint had not seen a sign of civilization except for the rutted dirt road he now followed.

"Any town out here can't be much," he said to his horse as he sat back down in his saddle, then lifted his reins and touched spurs to the flanks of his black gelding, Duke.

The gelding responded with more heart than was called for. Duke was a movin' kind of animal, only now he was missing a right front shoe and too many good feedings. The big gelding was plumb worn out, and since he was the Gunsmith's pride and joy, Clint was eager to get the horse to a good stable, where Duke could rest and recuperate. He'd have the black shod and curried back to a shine before he pushed on toward Denver Town.

This was a harsh country, Clint thought, seeing a group of Longhorn cattle off in the distance and noting how their ribs were showing even more than his own. Less than ten years before, it had been the stronghold of the fierce Comanche, but now that cattle were replacing the Indian and the buffalo, the land was being peopled by a few rugged frontiersmen and ranchers.

It was almost sundown when Duke's head lifted suddenly, pulling Clint out of a fitful doze. Clint shook his head to clear out the dust and cobwebs, and his gaze followed the horse's eyes to the north.

"Well, I'll be damned," he croaked in a dry, cracking voice. "It's got to be Huggins, and from the size of it, there's probably even a hotel, stable, and a saloon."

Duke's step quickened a little, and as the sun began to sink into the western horizon, Clint allowed the weary horse to gallop the last few miles into town.

Darkness was kinder to Huggins than daylight. The cracked and peeling paint on the storefronts was not apparent, and the horseflies and grime seemed to disappear. As Clint rode down the packed-dirt street, he counted about a dozen little businesses on each side. Each business had a porch, and most of them had a few chairs or benches in front for folks to sit and rest upon.

Actually, Huggins could boast two saloons, a weekly newspaper, one doctor, no church but a meditation society, and a blacksmith shop that also boarded horses at two bits a day.

Clint dismounted in front of the blacksmith's shop. It wasn't much, and normally he would not even have considered boarding his fine horse in such a seedy establishment. But there was little choice, and the first thing that Clint noticed was that the horses penned in a corral were all fat and looked well cared for.

"I'd hoped to get you a private stall, some fresh, clean straw, and plenty of oats," Clint said with a sad shake of his head. "But I guess life is full of disappointments for horses the same as for people. At least the hay looks to be of good quality."

"It is."

Clint turned around to see a tall, barrel-chested young man a few years younger than himself. The man was shirtless and had heavily muscled shoulders, thick forearms, and a bull neck.

"Are you the owner of this business?"

"I am." The man extended his hand. "Ben Bandy is the name. I can see that your horse has thrown a shoe and missed a few good feedings."

"You're a very observant man," Clint said. "How much do you charge?"

"Four dollars for a set of shoes."

Clint whistled. "That's mighty steep."

Bandy shrugged. "You want to do your own, that's fine with me. I got all the work I can handle in this town."

"How about board?"

"Two bits a night. Four bits if you want that fine animal grained and curried by a boy I have working for me in the mornings."

"All right," Clint said, knowing a man without alternatives was in no position to bargain.

"One thing, though," the blacksmith said, his voice taking on a note of warning. "I got a stud horse in that corral."

"So I noticed. He's a big buckskin."

"That's right. Mean as a snake. He belongs to a rancher named Pete Lane. Old Pete is gambling in town tonight, and I do him a favor in keeping the horse while he's visiting. But I sure don't like to keep a stallion among the other saddle horses. Especially one that bullies the other horses."

"What are you trying to say?"

Bandy studied Clint's horse. "Nothing except it might be best to tie your gelding up out here by the barn tonight. That way, he'll get the food instead of that buckskin stallion."

A faint smile appeared at the corners of Clint's mouth. "Let's put my horse out in that pen. After the hair quits flying, he'll want to have his fill and then lie down instead of being tied up all night."

The blacksmith looked doubtful. "Mister, I never seen a gelding yet that had the heart to stand up to a big stud like that buckskin."

"Get me a feed bag full of grain and let's settle this business," Clint said.

"Suit yourself," Bandy said with a shrug of his shoulders. "I figured I was just doing you a favor by giving you warning."

"I appreciate that," Clint said, whipping his stirrup over his saddle and reaching for the latigo tied to his cinch ring.

Clint quickly unsaddled Duke as Bandy unbridled the gelding and put on a feed bag filled with nutritious oats. Both men brushed the gelding, and it bothered Clint to see how Duke's ribs showed plainly in the lamplight.

"This big fella looks like a hell of a horse," Bandy said, stroking Duke's shiny coat.

"Best horse I ever owned."

"Fast as he looks?"

"Few faster," Clint said, "and I'm not bragging."

The blacksmith studied Clint over the horse's back. "You look familiar to me somehow. Have we met before?"

"I doubt it. I've never passed through this country." Clint chuckled. "And, if I can possibly help it, I never will again."

The blacksmith nodded. "I understand what you're saying. Me, I was born and raised here. My daddy and ma were killed and scalped by the Comanche when I was just a kid. I fought them many a time. Respect them, too."

"They're tough warriors," Clint observed. "So what keeps you here now? No offense, but this blacksmith shop isn't any prize. You could load up your supplies and go to Denver, Santa Fe, or a whole lot of other places and do better. Much better."

"I'm sure that's true," the blacksmith said agreeably. "But I got a girl that I'm sweet on that keeps me in these parts."

"Oh," Clint said, "that explains it. You gonna marry her?"

"Hope to someday. But hell, she don't even know that I'm alive."

"You'd best set about changing that," Clint said, thinking how the blacksmith was a fine figure of manhood. He needed a bath, a shave, and a haircut, but if he cleaned himself up real good, he'd be one to turn a country girl's head.

"How am I going to change myself?" Bandy asked.

"Well, you could start by taking a bath."

The blacksmith's eyes tightened at the corners. "You sayin' I'm dirty or that I stink?"

"No, no!" Clint said quickly. "Only that a girl likes a man that takes a bath once in a while."

"I wash up some. Working with horses isn't the cleanest occupation."

Bandy studied the manure and dirt crusted under his fingernails. "Mister, I'll never be a fancy man. And I guess if that's what it's going to take to win Miss Milly's heart, then I'll forever be a bachelor."

"There's plenty of women who'd latch onto a handsome young fella like yourself, clean or smelling of horse," Clint said, wanting to offer some encouragement. "Some of them might be a little smelly or dirty themselves."

"I wouldn't take no whore for a wife," Bandy said quickly.

"Oh, no," Clint said. "I wasn't thinking of that. It's just that there are fancy men and fancy women. Often, they sort of admire each other. Same for the other kind."

"Milly is kind of fancy," Bandy conceded. "So I just might be out of the runnin' altogether. Anyway, that's my problem. Right now, I think we can turn your horse into that corral if you're still of a mind."

"I am," Clint said, removing the empty feedbag.

He led Duke over to the pole corral, where Bandy opened the gate saying, "I'll pitch a few forksful of hay into the corral, but I'm still sayin' that the stallion will just gobble it all up for himself. He's a hog, that one, besides being a bully."

Clint turned Duke into the corral. Besides the big buckskin stallion, there was the normal assortment of saddle horses, about eight in all. None of them paid the new arrival any attention until hay was pitched into the corral.

The moment that Duke bent to eat, the buckskin stallion turned into a half ton of meanness and fury. It laid its ears back against its head and came flying across the corral to drive Duke away.

Instead, Duke whirled, planted his front feet on the ground, and kicked his back feet out like a pair of pile drivers. Clint winced when he heard the sound of Duke's ironclad hooves connect with the buckskin's muzzle. The stallion, its long yellow teeth exposed, ate Duke's iron shoes. Blood poured out of its mouth, and before it could recover, Duke whirled and bit the animal on the cheek, then shook the big stallion, tearing out a hunk of hide and hair.

"Jaysus!" Bandy swore. "Is that big sonofabich of yours half alligator, or what!"

"He's a prize, ain't he," Clint said, his chest filling with pride as Duke began to chase the bleeding stallion around and around the pen.

"Goddamn," Bandy swore again, "maybe we'd better get old Pete Lane's stallion out of there before that gelding kills him!"

But the Gunsmith grabbed the blacksmith's arm. "It'll be all right. My horse is just establishing a new pecking order, that's all."

Bandy didn't look too sure. "Pete Lane puts a lot of stock in that big buckskin. I'd sure be in his bad graces if your horse lamed or killed him."

"He won't," Clint pledged.

As if Duke had heard his master, the gelding gave up his

pursuit of the stallion and trotted back to the fresh hay. Nickering softly, the black horse began to consume the feed in great mouthfuls.

"I'd buy that horse for damn near whatever asking price you might name," Bandy said, his voice filled with admiration.

"Not for sale at any price," Clint said. "Duke has won me money in horse races when I was broke, and he's outrun Indians when I was bound to lose my topnotch if I'd have been caught. You can't put a value on a horse that'll keep you alive and in the money."

"You damn sure got that right," Bandy said.

Clint turned and cleared his throat. "I need a drink. I'll buy you one."

"I don't drink," Bandy said. "But plenty of the townspeople do. You'll have no trouble finding good company."

"And a game of poker?"

Bandy's smile faded. "I'm afraid Milly's father is gambling tonight again. Every time he goes into the Plains Saloon, he loses big money. You might watch out for him."

"What does he look like?"

"Big man, gray hair, and long handlebar mustache. He can get mean when he gets drunk. But sober, he's a fine man."

"I'll keep an eye on him," Clint promised. "But if a man wants to lose what he's got, that's his affair, not mine."

"I know," Bandy said sadly. "Trouble is, it's also Milly's business. It's just her and her father that's left—and their ranch. If old Pete loses that, Milly hasn't a thing in the world except a no-account brother that hasn't been seen in years."

Clint nodded and left the blacksmith. He would get a drink and see if there was anything he could do to look out for the old rancher. Then he'd go find a steak dinner and a soft bed for a good night's sleep.

TWO

It was almost ten o'clock before Clint wearily pushed into the Plains Saloon, wanting nothing more than a couple of cold beers and then directions to the nearest beefsteak. But the minute the Gunsmith walked into the room, he could smell trouble. After being a lawman for several years, a man developed a sixth sense about trouble; he could sense it instantly. Right now, Clint noticed that few of the saloon's customers were talking. There was a heavy silence, and everyone was looking toward a back table, where six men were playing a grim game of poker.

"A beer," Clint said, edging up to the bar.

The bartender nodded and quickly brought back a frothy mug. Clint waited for the bartender to say something, make some congenial conversation, but the man's lips were pursed and he wore a worried expression as he watched the card players.

"How much for the beer?"

"Two bits."

Clint laid down four bits. "For the second one," he explained.

"Uh-huh," the bartender said without interest.

"What's going on back there? Big game?"

"Yeah," the bartender mumbled. "I'm afraid old Pete Lane is about down to nothing but the clothes he's wearing and the title to his cattle ranch. And if he don't get up from that table and go home, he's going to walk out of here naked and without a roof over his head come tomorrow."

"Some men are real fools when it comes to cards," the Gunsmith said. "I've known fellas that were damn smart when it came to business, women, anything you could think of, but fools at gambling."

"That's old Pete," the bartender said, nodding in agreement. "He gets to drinking that mash whiskey and he loses all his sense. Figures he can still ride bucking horses, screw fast women, whip big men, and outgamble a snake like Art Bacon."

At Bacon's name, Clint frowned. "I know the man," he said. "We've crossed tracks a few times. I think he's crooked as a dog's hind leg. Slick, though."

The bartender agreed. "None slicker! Why, I'll bet he's already taken a couple of thousand dollars' worth of old Pete's cattle money. Third year in a row he's come to Huggins and fleeced Pete after his cattle sale. I just wish the sonofabitch would leave town and never come back."

Clint downed his beer in a series of quick gulps. He wiped his lips with the back of a dusty sleeve, then banged his mug down to signal he was ready for his second round.

"The way you swallowed that first one down, you must have had a powerful thirst on you," the bartender observed.

"I did. Is it always this dry and hot in these parts?"

"In the summer it is," the bartender said. "In the spring and the winter, though, it's a paradise. Pretty with grass as tall as the back of a horse."

Clint took his beer and moseyed on toward the back of the room. Art Bacon recognized him instantly, and when he did, the professional card sharp's hand froze in the middle of his deal.

Bacon was a name that fit, because Art was a hoggish man. He had jowls and little pig-eyes, deep-set and suspicious. His gut hung over his belt, and he had an undershot jaw and porcine lips. Art Bacon looked to be all suet.

He wasn't. Clint knew from experience that underneath all that fat there lived a powerful, extraordinarily cunning and quick man. Clint had seen Art Bacon draw and fire his gun with a professional's speed and accuracy. Bacon was also known to carry a hidden derringer on his person and had used it more than once to kill a disgruntled poker player.

"Well, well," Bacon said, forcing an ugly smile. "If it ain't the famous Gunsmith paying this little West Texas town a visit! To what do we mere mortals owe this great occasion?"

All eyes went to the Gunsmith, and everyone looked at him with sudden respect because he was well known all over the West.

Clint slipped his beer into his left hand and took a sip, his eyes never leaving those of Art Bacon. "I'm just passing through."

"Aww, what a cryin' shame," Bacon said in mock disappointment. "Too bad you can't stick around. Maybe we could play a hand or two for old times' sake."

"Maybe tomorrow evening," Clint said.

He shifted his attention to the other players, especially the old man who was staring at him through tortured, bloodshot eyes. He was so drunk he was trying to focus, and Clint had an immediate reaction of contempt. Pete Lane was too old and had worked too hard to allow himself to get drunk and lose everything he owned to the likes of a parasite like Art Bacon.

"You're Mr. Lane, aren't you?" Clint asked, forcing a smile he didn't feel.

The old man cleared his throat and threw his eyes around the room before settling them on Clint.

"I am."

"I hear you've got a fine ranch in these parts."

"That's right."

"And a fine daughter."

Lane's long handlebar mustache twitched. "And what business, sir, is that to you?"

"None at all, Mr. Lane. I was just thinking that a man with a good ranch and a fine daughter ought to be taking care of both instead of losing his money at the card table."

Lane pushed himself unsteadily to his feet. His face, moments before gray, now filled with red blood. "And what the hell is *that* supposed to mean?"

Clint knew men, and he knew that this one was dangerous and a fool. Pete Lane might be a hell of a fine man sober, but he was a man to be avoided when drunk. Clint knew the type, and he'd pistol-whipped more than one during his sheriffing days.

"It doesn't mean a thing, old-timer." Clint tipped his hat, gave Art Bacon a hard stare, and said, "If I were you, I'd take that big stack of chips in front of me, cash them in, and quit winners."

Bacon's lip curled. "But you aren't me, and neither are you the law in this town, Adams. That means that you're nothing more or less than a private citizen, and it also means that I can play cards or retire whenever I want."

Clint smiled a cold, deadly smile. "You always had a big bellyful of gut. And I've heard that you're as slick with that gun on your hip as you are in dealing from the bottom of a marked deck."

It was Art Bacon's turn to flush with anger. "You got no right to say a thing like that! Not without proof!"

"You're a four-flusher," Clint said. "You double-deal, mark cards, do every other thing but trust to skill and luck. And if I play you tomorrow evening and I catch you cheating, I'll nail your fat carcass to the wall with six bullets."

Bacon shook with anger. "I won't draw on you, Gunsmith. And if you try and push me around, I'll just take my money and find another card game."

"You've been warned." Clint glanced at the old rancher, who was watching him carefully. "And so have you, Mr.

Lane. A man of your position should acquaint himself with a better class of company."

Pete Lane blinked as if he'd been slapped. He had sunk back into his seat, but now he tried to jump up and caught his gun and holster on the chair. Clint left the old man struggling and cussing. Hell, if Lane wanted to throw everything he'd ever worked for in his life away, that was his business.

"One more beer," Clint said as he returned to the bar and stuffed his hand into his pockets for change.

"On the house," the bartender said, showing a nice smile. "If I'd have known I had someone famous like you in my place, I'd not have charged you for the first two beers."

The man returned a few minutes later with another beer. "Besides, Gunsmith, I liked what you had to say to old Pete and to that fat sonofabitch."

"If this is your place, why do you let men like that gamble at your table?" Clint demanded.

The bartender wiped the bar with a damp rag. "I dunno," he admitted. "I guess until someone catches Art Bacon actually cheating at cards and lives to tell about it, then the man has as much right to play as anyone else. I mean, it's like the law, isn't it? You got to prove a man is guilty before you can arrest him."

Clint grudgingly had to admit that the bartender had a point. "Maybe I'll stick around Huggins for a few extra days until I do catch Mr. Bacon cheating. I think that would be doing Texas a real big favor, don't you?"

"I sure do! And as long as that's your purpose, then drinks are on me. Seeing Art Bacon either run out of here or shot down by you would be the highlight of my week."

Clint chuckled and finished his third beer. "My belly is gnawing on my backbone," he announced. "Where can I find a steak dinner?"

The bartender pulled out a nice gold pocket watch. "I'm afraid all the eating places in town are closed up for the night. But if you aren't in too much of a hurry, I've got a little kitchen out back and I'll fry you a nice big steak. Got a table in the back room that I use to eat on myself. You can use it, compliments of the Plains Saloon."

"Why, that'd be real nice," Clint said. "Maybe I should go find myself a room at the hotel and then come on back."

"Do that," the bartender said. "Business, as you can see, is slow. Give me about a half hour and I'll have that steak on a platter."

Clint nodded with appreciation.

"In case you didn't notice when you rode into town, Huggins has only one hotel," the bartender said. "Four doors down on your right, this side of the street. Man who runs it is Bill Baker. He'll be reading in the lobby, and he goes up to bed and locks the door about eleven. Old Bill reads and rereads the same newspaper all week long until the next one comes out."

"Thanks for the hospitality."

"Think nothing of it. You tell old Bill that I sent you along. Be sure and tell him that you're the famous Gunsmith. That'll tickle the shorts off him."

Clint left the saloon, and less than a minute later he entered the Huggins Hotel. Sure enough, a little old man dressed in nothing but a pair of shorts and slippers was sitting in the lobby, reading a crumpled newspaper.

"Hello there," Clint said, removing his hat. "Man that owns the saloon said you might have rooms to rent."

"I got lots and lots of rooms," Baker said, squinting through a pair of square spectacles up at Clint. "How many you need?"

"Just one."

"Damn," Baker said, rolling to his feet and padding heavily around behind his counter. "I was hoping you'd take all four. How many nights?"

"I don't know for sure. Two at least."

"A dollar a night gets you clean sheets, a Mex woman to dust, and a hot bath in alkali water, to which we add a little gin to keep it from raising boils on your ass."

"Sounds fair." Clint dug two dollars out of his Levi's.

"Sign the guest book, please."

Clint signed his real name and Baker stared at it for an instant, blinking rapidly before he looked up and said, "Are you really Clint Adams? The Gunsmith?"

"A pretty tired Gunsmith. Yeah."

"Well, I'll be damned! From all the stories I've heard, I expected you to be about seven feet tall and three feet wide."

"You can't believe the stories people make up," Clint said with a weary smile.

Baker scuttled around the counter to stare at the Colt resting on Clint's hip. "Why, it ain't even tied down!"

"No," Clint said. "I can use it just fine where it sits. Besides, you tie a gun down, it hangs up on things like chairs, and when you're on horseback, your gun butt is sticking straight out behind you."

"Will you show me your fast draw?"

Clint shook his head. "I don't draw my gun unless I have damn important reason. A reason that has to do with living or dying. I'm sorry, but it's a rule I made a long time ago after seeing a drunk draw his gun and accidently kill his best friend."

"But you're sober."

"I am. And I'll need that room now, please."

Baker swallowed his disappointment and found a key. "You got room number one, first door on the right. You don't like it, there are three more to chose from. Two look down on the alley, two on Main Street. Take your pick. The only other guests are old Pete Lane and his daughter, Milly."

"A girl is staying up there?"

"She's got her own room. It's got a big lock on the door, and between old Pete and me, she's got nothing to worry about. I know you're a gentlemen, ain't you?"

"Oh, sure," Clint said quickly.

"Well, of course you are. All a famous man like you would have to do is snap his fingers and the women would come running."

Clint snorted. "I wish that were the case."

"You clean up a little," Baker said with a wink, "and you'd do just fine. All a man needs is a bath once in a while and you'll have yours first thing in the morning. A shave and a haircut wouldn't hurt you none, either."

Clint almost laughed, because it was exactly the same kind of lecture he'd given to the smitten blacksmith Ben Bandy. He guessed it had been like the kettle calling the pot black.

"Yeah," he said, rubbing the thick stubble on his chin. "I'll do that."

Baker winked. "You just mark my words if the women don't come running when they hear there's a famous and a handsome man staying here in this hotel."

With a self-deprecating wag of his head, Clint picked up his saddlebags and headed upstairs. Room number one was Spartan but clean, and it faced Main Street, which suited Clint just fine. He found a pitcher of water and a basin and removed his shirt to sponge himself clean with a washrag conveniently placed beside the basin.

A cracked mirror on the wall told the Gunsmith that Bill Baker hadn't been wrong: He was long overdue for a shave and a haircut. He'd get both tomorrow if they were to be found in Huggins.

Clint scrubbed the trail dust from his torso. Like Duke, he was a little on the thin side from too many miles of hard riding. There were dark circles around his eyes, and even to himself he appeared extremely fatigued. Maybe he'd stay in Huggins a few extra days and see if the heat subsided before pushing on to Colorado.

When he'd washed, Clint dried off and found a clean shirt in his bags. He was just pulling it on when he heard a short burst of gunfire and then shouting men. Clint hurried over to the window and pushed his curtains aside to stare down into the street.

He saw men pushing out of the Plains Saloon, and then one of them came rushing to enter the hotel. Clint turned back to open his door so he could hear better.

"It's old Pete!" a voice boomed from down in the lobby. "He drew his gun on Art Bacon and got hisself shot to death!"

Suddenly the door at the end of the hallway banged open, and in the rectangle of lamplight Clint saw a young woman. She was full-bodied, with long blond hair, and although he could not see her face clearly because it was in shadow, he could tell that she was pretty.

For a moment, she clung to the doorframe as if she were suspended there. "Daddy?"

Clint swallowed. He could hear footsteps coming up the stairs, and he knew that the girl was about to learn what she already suspected.

Bill Baker halted at the landing and looked down the long, dim hallway toward the girl. "Milly," he stammered, "I've got some bad, bad news."

"No," she breathed.

Baker and a man behind him pushed forward. "Milly, I guess you probably heard the gunfire," Baker said. "It was your father. He's . . . he's dead."

Clint heard the girl suck in a sharp breath, and then he heard her cry out like a wounded animal. She slumped to the floor and covered her face with her hands and began to sob hysterically.

Baker and the other man went to the girl and tried to console her, but Clint could see that they weren't going to do much good.

"Here," he said, pushing between the men to bend and scoop the crying woman up in his arms. He bulled his way through the doorway and laid her down on the bed.

"Miss," he said gently, "my name is Clint Adams. I'm sorry about your father."

"Who did it?" she cried.

"It was Art Bacon," the man beside the hotel owner said. "I saw it happen. Everyone in the room saw it. Your father finally lost your ranch, Miss Lane. He lost it, and then he went crazy. He drew first and even cleared leather before

Art Bacon went for his gun. I never seen a man any faster than Bacon. He killed your father with three bullets in the heart. Your pa didn't get off a single shot."

Milly's face crumpled with grief. "Then it was self-defense?"

"I'm afraid so," the man said. "Even though your pa was so drunk and wrung out from losing everything that he could barely get his gun up."

Milly seemed to get a grip on herself. "Where will they take his body?"

"I don't know."

"They can lay poor old Pete out in my lobby," Bill Baker offered. "I owe him that much."

"Thank you," Milly said. "And now, if you'll excuse me, I must get ready to receive my father."

All three men looked nervous. "Are you sure?" Baker asked.

"Yes. I'll . . . . I'll be down in a few minutes. Please don't let anyone in tonight."

"Why, sure," Baker said. "Except for the Gunsmith, who has room number one, you'll have your privacy."

"Thank you," Milly sniffled.

The three men left her alone and closed the door. The moment it was shut, they all heard the girl break down again, and her terrible sobs tore at their hearts.

"Damn," whispered Baker. "That's a fine, fine young lady. She deserved better than to be left alone without a single thing to her name. Old Pete used to be a real good man until the liquor made him crazy. He and I were friends for almost twenty years."

"I'll go tell the boys to bring the body over here and lay it down on the floor," the man who had come from the saloon said.

"No," Baker said. "Lay him out on the counter with a sheet over him. Comb his hair, wash off the blood, make him look as good as he could look. One time he was said to be the handsomest man in West Texas."

"Must of been a long, long time ago."

"Yeah, and before he lost his wife and started drinkin' himself to death."

Clint tucked his clean shirt into his dirty pants. He ducked into his room and grabbed his hat. Outside, in the hall, in his haste to go downstairs he almost bumped into Baker.

"Where are you going?" Baker asked in a distracted manner.

"I'm going to the saloon to have a few words with Art Bacon," Clint said in a tight voice.

"It was self-defense. Bacon is too smart to have done it any other way."

"Yeah," Clint said. "I'm sure he is. But I want him to know that he'll pay for this—sooner or later."

"I hope to God that it's sooner," the hotelman said, his voice filled with bitterness. "I know that it's hard to believe, but a few years back, Pete Lane was as fine a man as you'd ever want to meet. And maybe he could have been again if a snake like Bacon hadn't stripped him of his money and then taken his life."

Clint nodded. "I've seen men like Bacon all over the West. They're like vultures, or wolves. They see a man with something they want—something that he might have spent his entire life working for—and they go after it. They see his weaknesses and they go for the throat."

"That's Bacon's style, all right."

"I'm going to get him and the title to that ranch back," Clint promised. "I'll figure a way."

"He'd never be stupid enough to draw against you."

Clint took a deep breath and let it out slowly. "The trick," he said as he turned to go, "is to leave him no damned choice."

THREE

As Clint marched down the street toward the Plains Saloon, men stepped out of his path and then fell in behind. The Gunsmith could hear them whispering that he was going to go and kill Art Bacon. Maybe he was. Clint figured that Bacon was a man long overdue to be shot or hanged.

Pushing into the saloon, Clint saw a crowd of men gathered around the body of Pete Lane.

"What's everyone standing around for?" he lashed. "Bartender!"

"Yes, sir!"

"Get a wet towel and wash the blood off that man. Someone find a clean shirt. Clean him up and get him over to the hotel so his daughter can pay her respects."

The bartender jumped to Clint's command and found a wet towel. Clint moved around the end of the bar and helped himself to a bottle of whiskey. He poured a stiff drink and tossed it down with anger.

"Where did Art Bacon crawl off to?" he asked no one in particular.

"He didn't say," the bartender answered, coming back

around. "He just took off. Maybe he figured you were coming back."

"I doubt that's the reason he left," Clint said. "Bacon is too proud to show fear."

"Gunsmith?"

Clint turned to face a short, nervous man wearing a bowler hat and with an Irishman's pug nose. "What?"

"I watched him leave. He went to visit Madam Miles's house just down the way. Had a lot of money on him."

"Along with the title to Pete Lane's ranch?"

"Weren't no title. Old Pete, he just wrote it out on a napkin and had a couple of us witness the fact that it was servin' as a title to the Lane ranch. Probably ain't legal."

Clint poured himself one more drink. "I'm afraid you're wrong about that," he said to the men who were crowded around him. "Even though Pete was drunk and acting crazy, it was still his ranch and his right to sell it. Most judges take a man's gambling debts to be pretty important."

"Then you think he lost the ranch for his daughter?" one of the men asked.

"I think so, yes," Clint said, finishing his drink. "Point me to Madam Miles's house."

"End of the block, you turn right. It's behind the general store. Just a ramshackle place that used to be a livery. The Miles woman, she boarded up the roof and the cracks in the walls. Got three or four women that work for her."

"I've got the picture," Clint said, heading for the door.

Outside, the air was still warm and very still. Clint thumbed his hat back and gazed up at the glittering stars. He took a deep breath of fresh air, loosened his gun in his holster, and headed off down the street. Once again, men fell into his wake.

Clint stopped. "You boys go do your own business and let me tend to mine."

"You gonna shoot him down?" a man wearing a suit and starched collar blurted. "If you was to wait until morning and meet Bacon in the street, it would put Huggins, Texas, on the map. Be the biggest thing ever in this poor little town."

"Who the hell are you, the mayor and the Chamber of Commerce all rolled into one?"

"As a matter of fact," the man blustered, "I am running for mayor."

"Well, go campaign someone else," Clint said irritably. "I'm not of a mind to stage a gunfight for anyone."

"Might be we could make it worth your while if you waited until, say, noon. I think we could take up quite a handsome collection among the merchants and the—"

Clint took a menacing step toward the man and sent him into full retreat. Satisfied, the Gunsmith turned around and continued down the street.

Finding Madam Miles's house was easy enough because there was a big red lantern hanging over the massive front barn doors. The barn had no windows, and a small door had been cut out of the front wall. The door was standing wide open, and four horses were tied at a hitch rail in front.

As Clint moved toward the converted livery, he could hear the ribald laughter of both men and women. The Gunsmith frowned. Common sense told him it would be smarter and easier to seek out and confront Art Bacon tomorrow morning, when he was rested and there were no shadows where a hidden gunman might lurk. But the memories of Milly Lane and the sound of her racking sobs were too strong in Clint's mind to allow him to turn around, so he pushed on through the doorway.

No one paid him a bit of attention, and Clint stepped sideways and put his back to the wall while he sorted out his impressions.

Madam Miles's house was pretty damned humble, but Clint had seen a lot worse whorehouses in his time. This one had red lanterns hanging from cobwebbed rafters. There was a crudely constructed bar straight ahead, where a very obese woman stood, with most of her melon-sized breasts bulging out over a black crepe dress two sizes too small. She was pouring drinks and giggling with several customers. Clint had the impression that the fat woman was probably the madam. There was almost as much money to be made from watered-down liquor in this type of place as there was from the flesh. Most madams kept a close eye on the drinks and the money they generated.

Clint did not recognize any of the men. He looked in vain for Art Bacon, and then figured the man would probably be having his pleasure with one of the women. Hell, Clint thought, this is no place to have a showdown. Let's wait until tomorrow morning. Too many innocent people could get shot.

Clint was about to leave when a voice stopped him.

"Say mister, ain't seen you before in this place!" the fat woman shouted loud enough to be heard all the way back to the Plains Saloon. "Don't be bashful, step on over here and let me buy you a drink on the house!"

With a sigh of resignation, Clint ambled across the hard dirt floor.

"Well, well! If you ain't a handsome Jack! My, oh, my! I'm gonna have to beat my girls to keep 'em from all trying to climb on you at once. My name is Miles. Miss Lotta Miles. I own this establishment, and my girls are all clean and professional."

The woman stuck out her hand, and when Clint shook, it felt like he had grabbed a bunch of sausages. He pulled his hand away, unable to tear his eyes from the biggest breasts he'd ever seen on a woman. They were trophy-sized and might even have stirred some passion in him if it wasn't for a the fact that a vigorous growth of black hair sprouted from the canyon between them.

"Ha!" she said with a laugh that made all of her chins quiver. "You never saw anything the likes of 'em, have you!"

"Bigger than those of any range cow," he said, "that's for sure."

Lotta Miles laughed even louder, and then she hooked the elastic band of her neckline and yanked it down to expose fully the enormous breasts and nipples the size of conchos.

"Jaysus," one of the customers whispered, licking his lips, "you get a man's head between them, he'd suffocate!"

"Ha! Ha!" Lotta cackled, then grabbed the man by the ears and pulled his face between her enormous mounds.

Clint watched the poor sonofabitch in fascination as he struggled for air. The powerful woman held his face buried between her mountainous breasts for long several minutes, and when she released the ears, their owner toppled over over backward, gasping.

The whole place rocked with laughter, and Clint shook his head, backing a step to keep out of Lotta's grasp.

"Come on and drink up!" the big woman shouted. "Then look around and tell me which of my girls you'd like to give you the ride of your young life."

Clint took a drink. To his surprise, the whiskey burned like fire. He didn't even want to think about what had gone into the brew.

"I've come for Art Bacon," he said in a raw voice.

Lotta's smile froze. "You come to my place to see a *man*?"

Clint nodded. "Where is he right now?"

Lotta stopped smiling altogether. "Mister, why would you want to see a man when I've got girls willing to take you straight to paradise?"

"He killed a man less than an hour ago. Killed an old drunk right after he got him to sign over his ranch."

"You're talking about that crazy old Pete Lane, aren't you."

"That's right."

Lotta poured herself a drink. She looked at the pair of cowboys beside Clint. Refilling their glasses, she said, "Why don't you boys have a last drink on me and go home. You shot your wads. You spent your wages. Come back again next payday."

One of the men took Lotta's drink, downed it in a gulp, and said, "I sure wish you'd let us have one more round in the stall, Miss Miles."

The other man nodded hopefully. "Wouldn't cost you anything. A month is a long time for a man to have to wait for one of your girls."

"Then use the palm of your hands," Lotta snapped. "You will anyway."

The two men flushed with embarrassment, and it deepened when Lotta laughed in their faces. The taller of the pair might even have said something, except a big man who had been standing near Lotta moved closer.

The Gunsmith had heard and seen more than enough of this place. "Where is Art Bacon?"

"You want to kill him, do it someplace else," Lotta said.

"I want to see him," Clint replied. "Now."

The big man who was Lotta's muscle moved in beside his employer. He laid his hands on the bar and growled. "I think maybe you don't hear so good. Miss Lotta says that you need to either finish your drink and pay her for a girl, or else get the hell out of here while you can still walk."

Clint turned his attention on the man across from him. He was big and had shoulders like a bull. In his early thirties, he had a fist-busted nose, a terrible knife scar across his mouth that caused his lips to twist into a perpetual sneer, and dead-black eyes.

"Why don't you take a walk back into whatever shadow that hides your ugly face," Clint suggested in a quiet voice.

The muscle made a deep rumbling sound in his thick chest, and when he started to raise his hands from the bar, Clint pitched the dregs of his whiskey into the man's eyes.

"Ahhh!" he cried, covering his burning eyes.

Clint drew his gun, and when the man could see again, he was staring into a Colt .45 gun barrel.

"Leave him alone," Lotta ordered.

"Then tell me which stall that pig Art Bacon is rutting in," Clint ordered.

Lotta's face turned ugly with hatred. "Three stalls down," she said, jerking her thumb in that direction.

Clint nodded and holstered his gun. He moved off down the line of stalls that had been coverted into cribs. In each one he saw a mattress on the dirt floor and a couple fornicating or, in one case, just locked into an exhausted sleep. The place reeked of whiskey, vomit, sex, and sour sweat. Clint wanted nothing more than to get some fresh air.

At the third stall, he paused and stared into the dim shadows, watching as Art Bacon pounded up and down on some whore who grunted each time she was flattened by Art's great mass. All that Clint could see of the woman was her wide-spread legs, which were very thin.

Clint's mouth twisted down at the corners with revulsion. It would be just like Art Bacon, with his huge mounds of fat, to pick some skinny little whore he could bully and punish with his size. Right now, it sounded like she was being beaten with a fist.

"Finish up," Clint hissed.

Bacon twisted around, and although Clint could not see the man's face clearly, he heard the outrage. "What the hell you want? Seconds!"

"You killed Pete Lane. We're going to talk about it."

"Go to hell! It was self-defense!"

"So I heard."

"Mister, please!" the whore under Bacon pleaded, "can't you do this later? He's about to split me in half!"

Clint stepped back. His eyes were fully adjusting to the dimness, and he saw a very young girl, thin-faced and not very pretty, under Bacon.

"I'm sorry," he said. "Art, I'll give you three minutes. Don't try to run."

"Run!" Bacon laughed and then began to slam his thick body up and down so hard on the girl that Clint heard her begin to whimper like a puppy.

The Gunsmith turned away in disgust, hearing the poor girl beg for mercy and then hearing Bacon gasp in ecstasy as he finally completed his furious rutting.

Lotta was waiting for him at the bar. "I don't know who

you are," she said, "but you're not welcome back in my place
again. Get out!"

"Gladly," Clint said. "Just as soon as I have a little talk
with Bacon."

"Who are you?" the muscle hissed, looking for all the
world as if he were going to come over the top of the bar
and land on Clint with both feet.

"I'm somebody you don't want to tangle with," the Gunsmith said.

The man's big fist dropped beside the butt of his gun. He
glanced aside at Lotta. "You want me to take him, Miss
Miles?"

She studied the Gunsmith for a long moment, then shook
her head. "I don't think that would be such a healthy idea
for you, Don. Why don't we let this one go as long as he
promises not to come back."

Don looked almost relieved and Clint suspected that, like
many really big men, he was not all that quick. Very likely
Don had confidence in his fists and maybe a knife, but when
it came to shucking a gun with real speed, he probably realized he was no better than second-rate.

Art Bacon stopped in the middle of the room and began
to tuck his shirt into his pants. Clint noticed that the fat man
wasn't wearing his holster and gun.

"What do you want?" Bacon snarled.

"You killed Pete Lane."

"He was bad loser. Like I said, I killed him in self-defense
before a lot of witnesses."

"I hear it was no contest." Clint stepped closer to Bacon,
close enough to smell the rank juices of the girl he had just
made beg for mercy.

Bacon said, "A jury wouldn't spend five minutes finding
me innocent."

Clint focused entirely on the man before him. "I don't care
what a jury would say. I'm going to get that ranch back for
Milly Lane and see that your gambling career comes to a
sudden end."

"You threatening to kill me?" Bacon asked. He turned away to look at the other customers and then at Lotta Miles. "I think this man is threatening to take my life. And I'm not even armed. It would be murder, wouldn't it?"

The people around Clint nodded. Their faces were hard, and Clint knew that they would, to a man and woman, testify against him in Art Bacon's behalf.

"See?" Bacon said, licking his fat lips. "You'd better go away. People here don't like you."

Clint thought it a good thing that Art Bacon wasn't armed. The urge to kill this overstuffed vermin was about to overpower the Gunsmith.

"You've been warned," Clint said. "If you stay in Huggins, we'll face each other across the card table until you either lose all your money or you cheat and I have you dead to rights. If you refuse to play against me, I'll make you look like a coward, and you couldn't stand that."

"Then maybe I'll just go out to my new cattle ranch and wait for Miss Milly to come by," Art Bacon said in a mocking voice. "Maybe I could convince her that I'd be more fun in that cabin than her—"

Clint didn't hear what Bacon was going to say next. No one did, because the man's words were swallowed by the sound of Clint's fist driving up into Bacon's testicles and then of Bacon's scream.

The fat man grabbed his crotch and cursed, his voice high and shrill, like a woman's.

Clint turned on his heel and got the hell outside, where he could breathe. Maybe Bacon would go crazy and come after him with a gun. That would be just fine. It would just save them both time and trouble.

Back at the hotel, Clint stepped into the lobby to see Milly sitting in a chair, her pretty face buried in a silk handkerchief as she rocked with grief beside the body of her father.

Clint started to go past, but Milly raised her head. Her eyes were swollen and her voice barely a whisper when she said, "Did you . . . did you kill him, Mr. Adams?"

"Not yet, but I'm working on it."

Milly nodded. "Thank you. And if you change your mind about killing that man, please let me know."

"Why?"

"Because I will kill him instead."

"Oh."

Clint moved toward the staircase. "Good night, Miss Lane. I'm sorry."

"So am I." Milly sniffled. "Whiskey killed my father just as surely as Art Bacon's gun. Do you indulge yourself with hard liquor, Mr. Adams?"

"I do."

She shook her head as if this were a piece of tragic news. Not knowing what else to say or do, Clint turned his back on her and went up to go to bed.

FOUR

Clint slept until ten o'clock the next morning, when a knock sounded at his door.

Blinking the sleep from his eyes, he rolled over and lifted his gun from his holster, pointed it in the general direction of the door, and called, "Who is it?"

"Roy Marks, sir! I got hot water for your bath."

Clint climbed out of bed, stretched, and ambled over to the door. Being a naturally suspicious man, when he unlocked the door he made sure he was not standing flat-footed in the opening—just in case Art Bacon was paying Roy to set him up for a bullet.

"Sir?" Roy gulped. He was a thin, towheaded kid without shoes and with patches on the knees of his britches. "Sir, I ain't of a mind to get myself shot. Mr. Baker is only payin' me a dime to heat and bring up all these buckets of water."

Clint uncocked his six-gun and turned away. "Sorry to give you a start, boy. But a man can't be too careful when he has made as many enemies as I have over the years. Bring on the water."

"Yes, sir. Are you really the Gunsmith, sir?"

"That's right."

Roy gazed at him so steadily that Clint felt his cheeks warm. He turned and went back to pull on his shirt and heard Roy pour a bucket in a badly dinged tin bathtub with caulked seams.

"Got six more buckets of hot water comin'," Roy said. "Hot enough to boil crawdads."

"But not men?"

"No, sir!"

"Well, then bring them on in."

Roy didn't need further instructions. He poured all the buckets into the tub and then he stood around for a minute watching the steam rise and water seep through the caulking.

"Mr. Baker sure has got to get a new bathtub."

"I'd say so," Clint said, picking up his boots and stockings so they did not get soaked. "At least the water runs under the door and down the hallway."

"In this room," Roy said, "but not the others."

Clint tested the water. "Boy, that's hot!"

"You think it's hot on your shanks, just wait'll your balls boil in it," Roy promised as he watched Clint ease down into the tub slowly, a grimace on his face.

Clint could hardly wait as he eased down a little more and grunted, "Damn, that's hot!"

"Don't give up on it," Roy urged. "Real hot water like that will soak off the dirt fast."

Clint gritted his teeth and sank down to his waist, clenching his teeth to keep from howling in pain. Roy hadn't been exaggerating about boiling his balls.

"Ain't so bad after you're used to it, is it?"

"Next time make one of the buckets cold," the Gunsmith panted.

"Yes, sir. Anything else you need?"

Clint studied the ragged young scarecrow, then leaned out of the tub to grab his pants. He reached inside his pocket and retrieved a silver dollar. "You look like you could use a meal and a pair of new pants. Here."

Roy stared with huge eyes at the dollar that Clint spun over to him. "Oh, thank you, sir! But I'd never spend this."

"Why the hell not?"

" 'Cause it was yours! I'll keep it the rest of my life."

Clint frowned. Roy really did look hungry, and he was dressed in rags. "What if I gave you another dollar? Would you keep or spend it?"

Roy frowned. This was a very serious question.

"Close the door while you're thinking it out," Clint said with a hint of amusement making his eyes sparkle. "It's not good for a man to hurry on the tough questions he faces in life."

Clint's humor was entirely lost on Roy. "Well, sir," he said when the door was closed and Clint had holstered his gun and climbed into tub, "I'd have to admit that I'd spend it."

"Then dig another silver dollar out of my pants pocket and go spend it on something you need."

"I . . . I couldn't rightly do that, sir."

"Why not this time?"

" 'Cause I didn't do anything to deserve two whole dollars."

Clint scowled. "Tell you what. You can bring me up another bath tomorrow and . . . and you can curry my black gelding that's over at the livery."

"Still ain't near enough. Not for two dollars, sir. Not from a man like you."

"Well, it's enough for me! So it ought to be enough for you."

"Can I oil your saddle and bridle? Wash your saddle blankets and polish your boots?"

"Sure, but—"

"Then that'd make us square," Roy said enthusiastically. "That'd just be real fine all the way around."

"Good enough," Clint said, reaching for a bar of soap lying beside the tub but finding that Roy beat him to it first.

"Roy, what are you staring at?" Clint asked.

"Are those bullet wounds?"

"You mean this one in the shoulder and the other in my arm?"

"Yes, sir."

Clint nodded. "It comes with the job of being a frontier sheriff."

Roy sighed. "I sure wish I could have seen you when you fought some of the men you did. I heard that you gunned down the Pike brothers over in Tucson and they were all three pretty fast."

Clint looked away. It did not pleasure him to think back on the many gun battles he'd survived over the years. He was alive today because of luck and some skill and because he was a very, very careful man.

"Roy, don't even think of becoming a gunman. It's a job that will make you a lot of enemies and damn few friends. Even if you survive—and most don't—you'll never sleep as soundly as other men. You'll never walk in the evening without looking over your shoulder, afraid that someone might be taking aim on your back."

"But people look up to you. You should hear the talk in town about how fast you are. There's men all over town that have seen you gun down outlaws. They say you're the fastest man with a gun that has ever lived."

Clint shook his head. "Hand me that scrub brush over there, will you?"

"Yes, sir."

Clint soaped up the bristles and began to scrub himself vigorously. "If I had ever listened—and believed—that kind of foolish talk, I'd have been buried years ago."

"Want me to scrub your back, sir?"

"No, I can get it. You go spend that dollar. Get a good meal and a pair of pants. And a new shirt."

"All that for a dollar?"

"Take couple more," Clint said.

"But—"

"You can do something to earn the third dollar."

"What?"

"Keep an eye on Art Bacon for me. If he tries to leave town or it looks like he might be up to gathering some friends and coming over here to cut me down, then I want to be warned. Can you do that?"

"Yes, sir."

"Good. If you do that, you'll more than earn your money. Now get out of here."

Roy took his money and hurried away. As soon as the door was closed, Clint climbed out of the tub and puddled his way across the floor to lock it again. Yeah, he was a careful man.

Ten minutes later, just as he was enjoying his soak, a knock sounded on his door again.

"Who is it this time?"

"Bill Baker. I got a house key. Can I let myself in, or do you have company?"

"I'm taking a bath, but don't let that stop you," Clint said, thinking that, for all the privacy a man got in his room, he might as well have bathed downstairs in the lobby.

The key turned in the lock and Baker stepped inside, then relocked the door. "Howdy," he said, padding over to the bed, flopping down on it, and rolling his head sideways to regard Clint.

"Make yourself comfortable," Clint groused.

"Oh," Baker said, gazing up at the fly-specked ceiling, "I generally do."

The hotelman was silent for so long that Clint finally tired of waiting on him. "Did you come to tell me something, or just study the ceiling?"

Baker slowly rolled his head again and regarded Clint. "That boy scald your ass off?"

"No."

"Humph. I keep telling him not to bring the water to a boil, but he never listens. You can't believe how many times I've heard grown men howl up here when they've climbed into my bathtubs."

"Is that what you came in here to tell me?"

"That, and also that they're burying poor old Pete this afternoon at the cemetery. I figured you might want to come."

"Well, I don't. I didn't even know the man."

"Now, that," Baker said, "is sure going to disappoint Miss Lane. I hate to see that happen, on top of all the other disappointments she's trying to bear up under."

"Why should it matter to her if I come to her father's funeral?" Clint demanded. "I only met her father for a minute, and he wasn't all that friendly to me."

"Maybe not, but Miss Milly, she has sort of got it into her mind that you're going to get her ranch back and then take her to find her brother, Jackson."

Clint sat up straight in the tub. "What?"

"You heard me. She's counting on you."

"Well, I don't know why," Clint said. "I never promised her anything."

"Seems to me you did," Baker said in a lazy voice. "I mean, it was pretty plain that you went to Madam Miles's house to do more the screw her dirty old whores. Way I hear it, you buffaloed Don and challenged Art Bacon to a gunfight."

Clint groaned. "I just told the man that I wasn't going to let his killing Pete Lane pass without some retribution."

"Way I hear it told," Baker said, "you the same as challenged him to a gunfight, but he backed down."

Clint turned away. "How about throwing me that thing you call a bath towel but that a man wouldn't use to dry a dog."

Baker said nothing, but he got the towel. When Clint stood up to dry, the man went to the door, opened it, and said, "Miss Milly is sure going to be hurt if you don't come to her father's funeral."

Clint muttered an imprecation.

"Well," Baker said, standing in the doorway, "you want to break the last little pieces of that poor girl's heart, you go right ahead. Me, I'll be at her side come noon at the cemetery, just a few hundred yards north of town."

"You do that."

"I will," Baker said, slamming the door behind him.

Clint shaved and then dressed. He was clean, not too hungry, and well rested. He had planned to go have a nice meal, then wander over to the blacksmith's shop to see if Duke had gotten a good rest, too, and a new pair of shoes.

He'd planned to take a nap later, and come evening, go back to the Plains Saloon to see if he could rustle up a card game with Art Bacon. And if Bacon decided not to play cards, then Clint figured he would come up with some excuse to cross the fat man's path and goad him even harder.

Now, however, the thought of hurting Milly Lane's feelings was screwing up all of his plans and leaving him riddled with guilt. He went to his window and threw back the curtains. Directly below was the livery hearse, black even down to a pair of nice, matched horses.

A crowd was gathering, and Clint supposed that a funeral might be considered a pretty big social event in a little nothing West Texas town such as Huggins.

Even as Clint stared downward, he saw four men unload a very modest pine box from the hearse and then carry it inside. It sure wasn't much of a casket, but then, what difference did it make? Besides, Milly was no longer part of a ranching tradition. She was homeless and probably very low on money. If her father had ever had money, he'd probably gambled or drank it all up before his death.

Several women came over to console Milly, and Clint saw that they seemed to upset her. Twice Milly glanced up at Clint's window, and each time he stepped quickly back with a strong measure of guilt.

"Hell, girl, I didn't even know your father!" he railed at the curtained window.

But know him or not, Clint realized he did not have the heart to disappoint poor Milly. Cussing at his own weakness, the Gunsmith dressed quickly, and just as the pine box was loaded and the hearse about to be driven away, he hurried downstairs.

His appearance caused more than a little stir, and when Milly saw him, she actually managed what Clint supposed was a smile.

"Thank you," she said. "Thank you so much."

"Sure," he mumbled, taking her arm and escorting her over to the hearse.

"Would you ride beside me?"

Clint sighed. "But I didn't even know him. Surely there must be other men, friends of his that would be honored—"

"He lost most of his friends over the years of his drinking," Milly said. "And I know that he would have liked you very much."

Clint felt like a bug being drawn into a spider's web, but he couldn't stomach the idea of turning this pretty young woman down, so he nodded and helped her up onto the seat, then took a place beside her.

It was hot again, and in his coat and the tie he'd found to wear, he felt like he was suffocating. The cemetery was close, but even so, he was bathed in sweat by the time they arrived, and it didn't please him any to wait in the blazing sun while a couple of dissipated-looking Mexicans slowly finished digging the grave.

"I'm sorry there's no shade here," the mortician said, his own long face flushed with heat.

"Just plant him and make it a short sermon," Clint whispered so that the girl couldn't hear him.

The mortician did as Clint instructed. He said the Lord's Prayer and then gave a very brief eulogy. The minute the first spadeful of dirt was pitched, everyone was back in their wagons or saddles and heading back to town.

Everyone, that is, except Milly. She knelt beside her father's grave so long without moving that Clint began to think of her as a black statue.

Finally, the mortician, whose own face was bathed in sweat, leaned over and hissed, "You'd better get her out of the sun or she'll get a heat stroke and we'll end up burying her, too."

"Yeah," Clint said, moving over to take the girl's arm.

When she stood, she looked up at him and a fresh torrent of tears cascaded down her pale cheeks. "Please," she sobbed, "avenge my father's death!"

"I will," he promised.

She stopped crying, and her smile was suddenly radiant. "You will?"

"Yes. And I'll get the deed to your ranch back if I can trap Bacon into cheating at cards."

"Bless you!" she cried, wrapping her arms around his neck and kissing him full on the lips.

Clint would have liked to have responded, but since he was half-dizzy from the sun and filling his boots with sweat, he gently pushed the girl back and said, "Let's go."

She nodded. "When will you kill him?"

"I won't 'kill' him, as you put it," Clint explained. "My intention is to make him play cards and expose him at cheating, or at least win back your father's money and ranch. Failing both those objectives, I'll try to goad him into a fight."

"Put a bullet through his belly!"

Clint declined a reply. Instead, he led the girl back to the hearse and they drove quickly back to Huggins. Milly kept glancing sideways at him, and it made the Gunsmith a little nervous.

Just before they climbed down from the hearse, Milly said, "I hear you're going to Colorado from here."

"That's right," Clint said, reaching up to help the girl down.

Milly almost jumped into his arms and did so with such enthusiasm that Clint nearly tripped over his own heels and fell over backward. Again, he had to pry Milly's arms from around his neck.

"Yeah," he said when he had extracted himself. "I'm going to Colorado."

"I think I will, too, after this is over and you have killed

Art Bacon. You see, my brother, Jackson, is in Colorado—I think. I'll need him to help me run our ranch now that Father is gone."

"I suppose you will."

"Sure. A woman can't run a ranch alone. Not without a man."

"I wouldn't think so," Clint said absently.

"You ever do any ranching?" Milly asked, pinning him with the prettiest blue eyes he'd ever seen.

"Uh . . . no."

"Oh. Well . . . I . . . I bet you'd be good at it if you tried."

"I don't think so," Clint said, tearing his eyes from hers. "I like towns. I'm a gunsmith by trade."

"That's not what people in Huggins have told me. They say you're a fast gun."

Clint's brow darkened. "That's not true." He lowered his voice. "I was a sheriff for several years."

"And you killed every outlaw and fast gun you faced."

Clint sighed. "I have been very fortunate."

She looked down at the well-oiled, well-used Colt resting on his narrow hip. "And very good."

Clint could see that he was getting nowhere at all with this girl. "Here," he said, taking her arm and moving up to the hotel, "you've had a hard time, and I think it might be wise to go upstairs to your room and lie down."

She meekly nodded, and he led her into the hotel with half the townspeople of Huggins staring at them. Up the stairs they went, and when they reached the second floor, instead of going down to her room, Milly said, "Would you mind accompanying me into Father's room? He's got some things in there, and it would be very painful for me to be alone while I get them out."

"All right."

Clint followed her into Pete Lane's room. There really wasn't much in the room at all. Just a battered old repeating rifle, a canvas bag with a few personal items, and half a bottle of whiskey.

Milly stared at the bottle for a moment, then picked it up, opened the window, and hurled the bottle out into the street.

"Goddamn devil's brew!" she cried angrily.

"Here," Clint said, taking the bag and the rifle, "I'll carry these to your room."

Her expression softened. "Thank you."

When they were in her room, she laid her head against his chest. "I want you to know how much it means to me that you kill that . . . that animal that gunned down my father. It means more to me than getting my ranch back."

"You can't live on hatred," he said.

"I won't. When you've gunned Bacon down, I'll be fine again. You'll see."

She looked up into his eyes. "I want to go to Colorado with you."

"I don't think so," he heard himself say as he admired the contrast between the black dress and her blond hair. He had never understood why black was the color of mourning. It was his own opinion that black made women appear younger and more beautiful than any other color. Young, pretty women like this one dressed in black made Clint's heart pound a little faster and made his pants a little tighter in the crotch, though that was a pretty low-life thing to feel, much less admit, considering the circumstances.

"I'd better go."

"Are you going to hunt for him now?" she asked eagerly.

"No. This evening."

"Then maybe we could go to dinner."

"Are you . . . well, could you eat?"

"Of course. My heart aches, not my stomach."

"Okay, then, I'll come by and knock on your door at dinnertime."

"Thank you!"

Clint nodded and left her standing in her doorway. He had never seen anyone quite like Milly Lane. He knew that she really had loved her father and was grieving inside, but she sure wasn't it letting her stand in the way of her appetite or the need for revenge.

Strange and lovely woman, that. He'd have to be damned careful or she'd have him all bound up in her web so tight he'd never escape.

FIVE

Milly Lane stirred her coffee thoughtfully and gazed across the café dining table at Clint. "That was a lovely dinner, but I really wish you'd allow me to pay."

"Uh-uh," Clint said, leaning back in his chair and studying the pretty girl across from him. "So tell me some more about your father and the ranch he founded."

"Not much left to tell. It's not a big ranch, only about three thousand acres. In this country, it takes a lot of land to support cattle."

"So what do you suppose Art Bacon would do with it?"

"Sell it, of course. He's not interested in ranching. He'd just strip the land of its assets and sell it to the highest bidder."

Milly rested her chin on her folded hands. "I wish you had known my father when he was younger and Mother was alive. He was so full of life. He could work all day in the hot Texas sun, then ride thirty miles and dance half the night before starting home again. He was never cross or irritable. He didn't even gamble back then."

"Age and the loss of people we love can change us," Clint said. "Some men and women recover and go on to be happy again. Some never do. I've seen strong men turn bitter and weak, and weak men made strong by adversity."

"You look," Milly said, "like a man that's had more than his share of troubles."

Clint smiled with amusement. "Do I now?"

"Yes," she said, looking deeply into his eyes. "And I can't imagine you ever being weak."

He blushed a little. "I grew up in hard country where even the children learned to fend for themselves."

"Why did you become a lawman?"

Clint shrugged. "I can't say it was due to any one thing. I remember, when I was a boy of about ten, I did see a cold-blooded murder in our town. The man who was shot down was a minister, and he was trying to protect a poor Mexican. The men who shot him down gave no more thought to taking a good and innocent man's life than they would have to stomping a bug."

"And so you decided to become the protector of the weak. Is that it?"

"I guess," Clint said a little self-consciously. "Or at least I made up my mind that turning the other cheek was not for me. Maybe the minister is in heaven now, shaking his head at my ignorance, but I'll take my chances and stand up against animals like Art Bacon and his kind. With a badge, I could often even the score. There were laws, and I enforced them."

"So why did you quit?"

"I got tired of always looking over my shoulder. I got tired of having to face the next would-be fast gun. Sometimes he would be little more than a kid, and I'd almost get sick wondering if I could take the chance and try to wound rather than kill him. Some of those kids were terribly fast on the draw, and a few were just plain vicious."

"So you became a gunsmith?"

"I know and respect weapons, and so fixing them comes easy for me," Clint admitted. "I travel around the frontier, sometimes even in a wagon with all my tools. I meet people, repair their firearms, and when the kids come to me asking for advice on how to kill men, I give them a stern lecture against taking another human's life unless it is in self-defense."

Milly sipped at her coffee. "But . . . never mind."

"No. What is it?"

"I've asked you to kill Art Bacon. I've even asked you to kill him slowly. Now I feel ashamed of myself."

Clint frowned. "So you're wondering how I can preach killing only in self-defense and then, in the next breath, admit that I want to goad Bacon into a gunfight and kill him. Is that it?"

"Yes. You're saying one thing, practicing another."

"That's true," Clint admitted. "But, you see, I *know* Art Bacon. I've seen him in action before, and he's a killer. He has gunned down too many men over a deck of cards, and he's so fast on the draw and so cunning that he always waits until the other fellow makes the first move. He also makes certain that there are witnesses. That way he can never be arrested or tried for murder."

"But it *is* murder!"

"Of course it is. Your father never had a chance."

Milly's eyes glistened with tears. "He deserved to die in a noble manner. Instead, he was gunned down in a damn saloon."

Clint said nothing because there was nothing he could say. The thought had entered his mind that old Pete Lane might have wanted to die. Certainly he'd been trying to drink himself into an early grave, and he might just have decided, in his pain and confusion, to have his life end very suddenly.

Clint looked over at the clock on the counter. "I think I'd better take care of business."

Her eyes widened. "You mean with Bacon?"

Clint nodded, his expression wintery.

"Maybe you shouldn't," she blurted. "I couldn't live with myself if something happened to you."

"It wouldn't be your fault." Clint pushed back his chair and stood up. "I'm not doing this entirely for you, Milly. I'm doing it for the next man and the next that Bacon will gun down if I don't stop him."

She came to her feet and nodded, her chin dipping just once and her eyes on his face.

"When it's over, will you come knock on my door?"

"It might be very late," he hedged.

"I don't care. I won't sleep anyway. I couldn't sleep knowing that you might be killed. Please."

"All right," he said, "but it could be that nothing will happen tonight. Bacon is smart. He's not going to allow himself to be goaded into a stand-up gunfight with me. He only uses his gun when the odds are all in his favor."

"Stop by anyway."

"Okay."

Clint escorted Milly back to the hotel, and when he started to turn toward the saloon, she grabbed him around the neck and kissed his mouth.

"What did you do that for?"

"For luck," she breathed.

He smiled, tipped his Stetson to her, and said as he left, "Everyone can use a little luck."

When Clint entered the Plains Saloon, the bartender looked up suddenly, then all conversation died. Clint pretended not to notice as he strolled over to the bar and ordered a whiskey, his eyes glued to the back table where Art Bacon and several others were playing cards.

"I wish you'd settle this somewhere else," the bartender hissed under his breath.

Clint took a drink. "I just come to play a friendly game of cards. Nothing wrong with that, is there?"

"Why don't you play some other time or place?"

Clint's eyes locked with those of Art Bacon. "I don't think it would be as interesting," he said as he moved toward the back of the room.

"Mind if I pull up a chair and sit in on a few hands?" Clint asked with an easy, friendly smile.

There were five other players besides Art Bacon, and they all shook their heads. Bacon, however, said, "Table is full. Sorry."

Clint reached out, grabbed one of the players by the front of his shirt, and jerked him to his feet. "I guess you're done for the night, huh?"

"Yes, sir!"

Clint let the man go. He smoothed the man's rumpled shirt and smiled. "Thanks."

Bacon looked like a man ready to eat horseshoe nails when Clint sat down, grinned, and extracted a roll of greenbacks from his pocket.

"What's the ante, gentlemen?"

"A dollar," one of the players growled.

"A dollar it is. And what's the game?"

"You'll find out when I decide myself," one of the players said as he took the cards, shuffled, and began to deal.

The game was seven-card draw, and for the next three hours it didn't vary much at all. Clint played well but conservatively, and he managed to make thirty dollars by midnight.

Art Bacon, however, was having a real run of good luck. He'd relaxed after the first hour and even began to enjoy himself as the money in front of him grew steadily. Two of the other players quit shortly after midnight but the other two hung in there despite losing steadily. Every time Clint thought they were tapped out, they'd drag another wad of bills from their pockets and keep on playing and losing their money to Bacon.

The pair didn't seem to mind, though, and it took Clint a while longer to realize that the pair were in cahoots with Bacon. They pretended not to be, but a few times their eyes locked with Bacon's in an unmistakable question.

Clint reassessed the situation because, most likely, the fat man had hired them to help kill him. And since the hour was late, it seemed pretty likely to Clint that whatever happened was going to happen very soon.

"Three kings," Clint said as he scooped up a pretty large pot and pulled it toward him.

"Whoa up, now," Bacon warned, fanning his cards on the table. "I've got a flush. Too bad."

Bacon started to reach for the pot, but Clint's words stopped him cold. "Turn over the deck, and everyone lay their cards face up."

"What?" the other two men hissed.

"You heard me. I want to see every card played—and unplayed."

Those who remained in the saloon shifted nervously, and the silence became so profound that Clint could hear his own heart beat. He pushed back from the table.

"Turn 'em face up, boys. Now!"

A blue vein began to throb at Art Bacon's temple. "You saying there's cheating going on here?"

"Just show me the cards and we'll see what we'll see."

But Bacon shook his head. "You know a man can't stand to be treated like that. Not and call himself a man."

"You got a choice," Clint said. "Turn your cards up or lose the pot."

Bacon shivered with pent-up fury, but under Clint's steady gaze he curbed his impulses and spat, "You can take the pot. I'm out."

"Me, too," the other two men said, coming to their feet and being real careful to keep their hands away from their guns.

The two men started to pocket their money, but Clint said, "Leave it on the table."

"Huh?"

"It all belongs to him, doesn't it?" Clint said, tossing his eyes at Bacon. "He's the one that's paying you."

"Now, wait a damn minute here, mister! We ain't—"

The back of Clint's hand cracked against the man's jaw and sent him reeling. The man cursed and went for his gun. Clint drew his Colt and fired in one smooth motion. His bullet shattered a button, driving pieces of wood along with lead into the hired gunman's heart.

In the next instant, all hell broke loose. Out of the corner of the Gunsmith's eye he saw a two-shot derringer materialize in Art Bacon's pudgy hand. Clint tried to spin around and fire, but the derringer barked first, a sharp, angry sound. Clint felt as if a mule had kicked him in the side. He was knocked halfway around, which probably saved his life, because the second bullet from the derringer just plucked at his shirtsleeve.

Clint dove for the floor, his six-gun bucking lead. He drilled the second man from the floor, his bullet catching the man just under his jaw and exiting through the back of his skull.

"Damn you!" Bacon roared as he hurled the derringer away and dropped downward for his six-gun. The Colt seemed to jump from his holster as if it were a live thing. Clint rolled and fired in the same instant as two guns exploded in unison. Clint felt sawdust spray his face as he kept pulling his trigger, making Art Bacon dance an almost comical minuet of death.

The hammer of Clint's gun dropped on an empty cylinder, but the fat man's gun burped one more bullet into the sawdust-covered floor. Clint looked up and saw Bacon's eyes glaze, and then the huge man delicately cradled his protruding gut as if it were a treasure chest of jewels. All at once blood began to leak from between Bacon's bloated fingers, and the man stared at it with a look of dazed wonder before he toppled, spintering a chair beneath him. When he struck the floor, a great whoosh of fetid air blasted from his lungs.

The Gunsmith climbed to his feet and with a tight smile began to turn over all the cards.

"Six spades is what I count," he said at last to no one and everyone in the hushed room. "Anybody else see it different?"

The patrons edged cautiously up to the table and, one by one, shook their heads.

"I'd say that Art Bacon has been cheating all along."

Clint removed his hat and swept the money into his black Stetson. "Boys, I'm taking up a collection for Miss Milly Lane. Is there anyone who *doesn't* want to contribute?"

No one dared not contribute, and while the men filed by, tossing money into Clint's hat, he bent and rummaged through Art Bacon's pockets. Finding the napkin with the scrawled deed to the Lane ranch, Clint tore the paper to shreds and sprinkled them ceremoniously over the massive body of the dead killer.

"Here," the bartender said, coming up to Clint with a wet towel, "better let me take a look at you."

Clint was feeling a little weak, so he sat down and unbuttoned his shirt.

"It's just a scratch," he said, looking down at the bartender wiped the blood away to get a better look at the bullet wound in his side.

"It's more than a scratch," the bartender said. "But you'll live if we can stop the bleeding."

Clint pressed the towel hard against his side. He pulled twenty dollars from the hat and gave it to the bartender. "Drinks on the house as long as that lasts."

The bartender grabbed a bottle, a clean shot glass, and some more towels to be used as bandaging. When he returned to Clint's side, he shook his head in wonder.

"Mr. Adams, you are one hell of a shootist, aren't you? But you also got some strong luck running in your favor."

As the men crowded around him and began to offer congratulations and pat him on the back, the Gunsmith wearily nodded his head in agreement and tasted sweet Milly Lane's earlier good-luck kiss.

"I had some luck, all right," he told them. "And I know where I can find a little more before the night passes."

No one understood his meaning, and maybe that was just as well.

SIX

Milly Lane answered his very first knock at her hotel room door. "Is that you, Clint?"

"Yes. I just want you to know that Art Bacon is dead."

Clint heard Milly's sharp intake of breath, and then as he was turning to go to his room, Milly flung the door open and threw herself into his arms.

"Oh, Clint!" she cried. "You did it!"

"Ouch," he said, because she was squeezing his injured rib.

Milly stepped back and then noticed the wet bulge under his shirt. "You've been shot!"

"It's just a flesh wound," he told her. "I think the bleeding has stopped. At least it was until you gave me a squeeze."

"Oh, I'm so sorry." She grabbed his arm and pulled him into her room. "Sit down on the bed and let me take a look at it."

"I already have. It looks nasty, but it didn't even nick the rib. I'll be fine, Milly."

"I'm not sure you're capable of making that decision," she told him a little sternly. "So pull off your shirt and let me take a look."

Clint did as he was told and then watched as Milly gently removed the bar towel and made a grimace. "Bacon's bullet?"

"Yeah. He got me with a hidden derringer. I should have been ready for it, but I was a little busy with his two friends."

She paled. "Two friends?"

"That's right. Bacon wasn't the kind of a man who worried about fighting fair. He liked big odds in his favor. I had to whittle them down a mite before I got around to him."

Milly passed a hand shakily across her eyes. "My dear man, if I'd have suspected that Bacon would have a couple of men to help him, I'd have done everything in my power to persuade you not to go into that saloon."

"I would have gone anyway," Clint said. "The man had lived much too long. And by the way, I found that napkin that your father used to sign away his ranch."

Clint paused.

"And?"

"And I tore it to shreds," Clint said with a grin. "I told everyone that since I'd caught Art Bacon cheating, all bets were off. There were no objections. And there's one other little thing."

Before Milly could ask, Clint removed his hat and laid it brim-high on the bed. When Milly saw it was stuffed with greenbacks, her eyes grew wide. "What is that for?"

"The boys at the Plains Saloon took up a little collection for you, Milly. I guess they understood that your father deserved better than he got. So they wanted to help you out."

Tears welled up and then slid down Milly's rosy cheeks. "Oh, Clint!" she wailed. "I can't thank you enough!"

"Hell," he said, "you don't have to thank me."

She sniffled. "But I want to. I want . . . I want to be very special to you, darling."

Clint raised his eyebrows in question as Milly slipped back into his arms and kissed him passionately.

"Milly," he said, a weak protest in his voice, "you've just

lost your father and maybe you aren't thinking straight yet.
I think—"

Whatever the Gunsmith was thinking changed dramatically when Milly unbuckled his gunbelt and then his pants. He
blinked and chuckled softly as her warm hand slid down to
caress his flaccid manhood.

"You've been shot," she whispered in his ear, "and I don't
want to overburden you physically, but if you think you are
up to it, I'd like to know you as a man, Clint."

"Whew," he breathed, feeling himself get "up" to it as her
fingers sent shivers up and down his spine. "Whatever you
say, Milly."

She sat up quickly and began to undress. Clint was surprised to see that she wasn't wearing a stitch of underclothes
under her dress. And if he had expected her to be shy or a
bit modest, he was surprised again because when Milly was
fully undressed, she shoved out her chest.

"Do you like them?"

"They're beautiful," he said, meaning it because her breasts,
while not huge, were firm and very enticing.

She stood up and helped him remove his boots, and then
she yanked off his pants. Studying his now stiff manhood,
she licked her lips and sighed.

"Even all shot and scarred up, you're the most beautiful
man I've ever had."

"Have you had many?" he asked, then almost instantly
regretted the question.

"I've had six, but three of them were just boys I knew
when I was young. So I've only had two real men. Neither
of them was as pretty as you, Clint."

Clint pressed the wet bar towel to his side so that if
the action got too frenzied, he wouldn't bleed all over the
mattress.

"Come on," he said. "It's your room and your party."

Milly climbed astraddle him and grabbed his manhood,
then spread her legs wide and began to rub it gently against
herself.

"Ohh," she sighed, rolling her head back on her shoulders and parting her lips, "you won't make this happen too soon, will you?"

"I'll try not to," he promised.

"Good."

Milly had a tight, muscular little bottom, and she began to rotate it around and around on the tip of Clint's manhood. It was exquisite, and Clint moaned with pleasure as he laced his fingers behind his head and closed his eyes.

"Like it?" she panted.

"I sure do. Don't stop."

Milly didn't stop. For almost a quarter of an hour, she worked her bottom over Clint's throbbing tool. Sometimes she would ease down and impale herself, then wiggle like a bunny before she'd gasp and raise up again, only to start the process all over again.

"I don't know how much more I can stand of this," Clint said, unlacing his fingers and reaching down to grab each of Milly's firm buttocks. With a hard pull and accompanying thrust of his hips, he drove himself into her all the way.

She shivered and collapsed, dropping forward at the waist to lave his nipples with her tongue as he began to piston his manhood.

"Oh, Clint," she said in a trembling voice. "It was never like this before. Never!"

"Glad to hear that," he said, feeling as if he was going to explode at any moment.

"Oh!" she cried, suddenly kissing him furiously. "Oh, darling!"

Clint felt her insides tighten, and then she began to milk him furiously. With his own loins on fire, he rolled her over and began to slam his thick rod in and out as hard and fast as he could. A moment later, he lost control of himself and felt as if a river of fire were passing from his body deep into that of the squirming young woman.

It was several minutes before they caught their breath and the Gunsmith rolled off of Milly.

"Was it good for you, too?" she asked.

"It doesn't get any better," he admitted. "I could have been bleeding to death, and I wouldn't have been able to stop."

She bent down and looked at the bar towel. "It's fine. No more blood. You're going to be stiff tomorrow in more ways than one."

Clint understood her double meaning. "Aren't you a little concerned about your reputation in Huggins?"

"What do you mean?"

He pushed up on one elbow. "Well, you know. I was just thinking about what the townspeople would say and think if they realized we were making love. I'm afraid it would go hard on you."

Milly sat up cross-legged and leaned her elbows on her knees. Looking at her now, Clint thought she appeared to be a little girl. Only the slow burn in his loins told him she was very much a grown woman.

Milly sniffled. "They say there are only two kinds of women out in the West: the good and the bad. I never accepted that. Do you?"

"No. I've seen 'good' women, if you define them as the ones that are married to respectable men and trying to raise families, go bad. And I've seen 'ladies of the night' or 'soiled doves' who were as kind as virgin saints. You can't judge a man or a woman by their circumstances. A lot of bad men and women live very well."

"I agree," Milly said. "And I'll tell you something else. When my father became a drunkard, the people in Huggins who were once his friends turned their backs on him. The same thing happened to my only brother, Jackson. He couldn't stand the gossip and the pity, so he up and left, cursing the whole town."

"People can be hard."

"You can say that again," Milly said with more than a little anger. "Girls I grew up with suddenly looked away when I passed them on the street. So I don't give much of a damn what anyone in Huggins, Texas, thinks of me."

"You might someday," Clint said. "Especially if you rebuild your father's ranch."

"I wish you'd help me. I'd like to take you out there tomorrow. Maybe if you see it you'll decide to stay."

"I'm sure it's pretty," Clint said, "but ranching just isn't my line of work."

"But you could learn!"

"Possibly, but I don't want to learn. I like traveling from town to town and meeting new people. I like playing poker and fixing guns and swapping lies with the people I meet. I'd never be happy tied down to a ranch."

Milly had been looking deep into his eyes. "Yes," she said with resignation. "I can see that you mean what you say, and I'm sorry."

"So am I. It isn't every day that I get that kind of an offer from a girl as beautiful as you, Milly."

"Beautiful, but lonely."

"Ben Bandy worships the ground you walk on."

Milly smiled. "He tell you that?"

"Yep."

"Hell," Milly said, "he's had a hard-on for me since we was both in diapers."

It was Clint's turn to laugh. "Can you blame him?"

"No. But I don't have to love him back, do I?"

"Not if you don't want to," Clint told her. "He just strikes me as being a damn good man with horses. I'll bet he could learn to run cattle as well and make a fine rancher and husband."

"He smells like horse all the time."

"I told him to wash and clean up more."

Milly chuckled. "What did he say to that?"

"Said he'd give it some thought. I think he'd do most anything to win your heart, Milly."

She sighed. "Why is that people are always attracted to people that aren't attracted to them? Look at me lookin' at you like you were a piece of candy I wanted to gobble up. And poor old Ben Bandy walks bowlegged every time I step into his livery to get a horse shod." Milly shook her head. "I tell you, none of it is fair!"

Clint smiled. He reached out for her and drew her into his arms. "I'm going to Colorado. If you want, you can come along and we'll hunt for your brother."

"It might take a long time to find Jackson," she warned. "He's wilder than a Texas tornado."

"I'm in no hurry." Clint traced a forefinger around her nipple and watched it stand up hard.

"You wanting more of me already?"

He looked down at himself and saw that he was growing long and stiff. "Yep."

Milly clucked her tongue in admiration. "Boy, oh, boy," she whispered, coming into his arms. "I guess I had all boys before now. Either that, or you're half stallion."

"All stallion," he said, rolling her onto her back and pushing her silken thighs wide apart. "All stallion."

Then Clint mounted the pretty young woman and slipped his right hand under her firm buttocks.

"Before you start," she panted, "I got to know something."

"All right."

"Do you think there are other men like you out there someplace? I'd just kill myself if there weren't."

Clint had to laugh at that, but when he looked back down at her and saw that Milly was dead serious, he said, "Girl, when you find a man that you really love, he'll satisfy you even better than I can."

"Uh-uh," she moaned, her hips stirring under his. "I'll never believe that."

Clint didn't think that he cared to argue the point, so he closed his eyes and they moved against each other in a slick, satisfying union. When the pleasure of it became so intense that his mind began to scatter, the Gunsmith again brought her to a powerful climax and then filled her with another torrent of his hot seed.

SEVEN

It was much later in the morning than Clint had intended when he and Milly finally arrived at Ben Bandy's livery.

"I see you got around to shoeing Duke," Clint said with approval as he inspected his horse's hooves. "It's a good thing, because we've got a long trail ahead of us."

"Yes, sir," Bandy said, a questioning frown wrinkling his brow. "Are you and Milly figuring to go someplace today?"

"We're heading for Colorado," Milly said happily. "We're going to find my brother, Jackson."

"What for?"

Milly's smile slipped. "Why, he's my brother, ain't he? And now that Clint has got the title to my ranch back, I need Jackson's help."

"Milly," he said, "Jackson and I were pretty good friends all during our growing years, and I know him real well. I don't think he's the kind of fella that will want to come back and tie down to your ranch."

"That's not true!"

"It *is* true," Bandy said stubbornly. "Your brother is just too wild for settling down on that ranch. He wouldn't last a month."

"Sure he would! And he's a top hand."

"Oh," Bandy said, trying to be diplomatic, "Jackson can fork a bronc like no man I ever saw, and he's as good with a rope as a vaquero, but he don't take to long hours of hard work."

"Ben Bandy, are you trying to tell me that my own brother is lazy?"

"No, ma'am!" Bandy threw a beseeching glance at Clint, but the Gunsmith figured the man had put his own foot in the cow plop and was going to have to get it out himself.

"Well, then?" Milly demanded, hands resting on her shapely hips, "just what are you trying to say?"

"Only that Colorado is a long ways to go for a man who might not even come back and, if he doesn't, sure wouldn't stay."

"You make me so damn mad," Milly said, actually stamping her boot down in the dirt, "and from way back to when we was kids, you always were trying to tell me what to do. I didn't listen to you then, and I damn sure won't listen to you now."

"Well, if you had. . . ." Bandy bit off whatever he was going to say in midsentence. "Aw, the hell with it!"

Clint thumbed back his Stetson. "If you boys and girls are done arguing, we're going to need to buy a packhorse. What have you got for sale, Ben?"

Ben's expression was bleak when he turned away from Milly and shrugged. "Come on over here by the corral. I've got two or three that ought to do."

Clint was plenty glad to look at horses instead of listen to Ben and Milly argue.

"I could let you have that chestnut gelding with the two white stockings, or that little bay mare, or the sorrel with the blaze on his face."

"What are you asking for them?"

"Thirty-five dollars for the chestnut, twenty-five for either of the other pair."

"Ben Bandy, that's outrageous!" Milly exclaimed. "Why,

I thought you were my friend, and here you are trying to get rich all at once at my expense."

"Get rich? Get rich?" Bandy bellowed. "Why, I'm practically giving those horses away at the prices I just quoted. You don't want to pay the asking price, then go find yourself someone else's horses!"

Bandy started to stomp away in anger, but Clint caught the man and said, "Whoa up, there! We need a good packhorse and packsaddle. We'll pay your price on the chestnut if you throw in a packsaddle."

"Why should I do a fool thing like that?" Bandy demanded. "The only packsaddle I have is worth ten dollars at least."

"Well, I'm not paying it!" Milly called.

"Then I'm not selling it to you!" Bandy shouted.

Clint groaned with exasperation. "Damnit, will you two quit fighting! Milly, if the saddle is any good, it's worth at least ten dollars."

"Then you buy it, 'cause I won't."

"I wouldn't sell it to you now, anyway!" Bandy shouted.

"All right!" the Gunsmith shouted. "Enough! I'll buy the damn saddle. Milly, you pay Ben for the chestnut and let's get this show on the road for Colorado before I wash my hands of the both of you and go it alone."

Milly actually paled a little at this threat. "You promised to take me along and then to help me find my brother."

"And I'll keep my promise," Clint said, "but nothing was said about having to put up with listening to you and Ben quarrel like a couple of schoolchildren."

"I'll get the packsaddle," Ben snapped, marching into the barn stiff-backed.

"I thought you said he was attracted to me," Milly complained when the young blacksmith was out of hearing distance.

"He is," Clint groused.

"Well, he sure don't act like it to me," Milly said. "And he ain't cleaned himself up or taken a bath since the last time I saw him."

Clint was fed up with both of them, and he clamped his jaw shut until Ben came out lugging a good packsaddle. The blacksmith dropped it at Clint's feet and said, "You're stealing it at ten dollars."

"Then don't sell!" Milly said angrily.

"Quiet!" the Gunsmith growled. He took ten dollars out of his pants pocket and paid for the saddle. "I'm obliged to you for giving me such a good deal. We'll need a good saddle and packhorse. Pay the man thirty-five dollars for that handsome chestnut, Milly."

She paid him.

"Thank you. How about your own horse, Milly? Has he been shod lately? If you're going all the way to Colorado, you'd best start out with a fresh pair of shoes."

"We need to get going," Clint said, growing impatient.

"You won't save any time if Milly's horse throws a shoe and goes lame," Ben argued. "Better let me have a look."

"He's right," Milly said. "And I don't think my horse has been shod in months."

Clint sighed. "All right. In the meantime, I'll saddle Duke and the packhorse and get supplies loaded."

He glanced up at the sun. "Hell, it'll be afternoon before we finally get out of Huggins."

"Bring your horse on over, Milly," Ben said quietly.

"What are you going to charge me?"

"It'll be free," Ben said. "Sort of for old times' sake."

Milly's blue eyes widened. "Ben, I won't take charity. Besides," she said, pulling out the big wad of money that Clint had taken up as a collection the night before, "I've got the means to pay for what I need."

"Keep it for the trail," Ben said, turning away to get his forge stoked up hot so he could make the shoes for Milly's horse.

Clint heard Milly swear in a most unladylike way as he headed for the barn to get his saddle.

It took the Gunsmith less than an hour to get all the supplies they'd need for the long trip to Colorado. At the general store he bought extra ammunition and plenty of food along with a few extra blankets, knowing it could get cold at night in the higher elevations.

"Put everything into two canvas sacks and load them on that chestnut toting that packsaddle," he told the store owner.

"You look to be heading a fair distance," the man said.

"Colorado."

"What for? We got everything you need right here in Huggins."

"Not quite," the Gunsmith said. "Besides, I'm off to find Miss Lane's brother, Jackson."

The owner had been loading the supplies, but now he stopped and straightened. "You're going to bring him back?" he asked with a frown.

"I'm not bringing anyone back. Milly is. She's going to need help on that ranch now that her father is gone."

"Well, sure she will, but Jackson is more hindrance than help. He's too damn wild to work at anything."

"So I've been told," Clint said. "But that's Milly's problem, not mine."

"If you find Jackson, mark my words, he'll become *your* problem," the man predicted solemnly.

Clint just frowned. Everyone seemed to share the same poor opinion about Milly's wayward brother. It made him think that looking for Jackson was not only a waste of time, but also a mistake.

When he returned to the livery, Ben was just finishing up tacking a new set of shoes on Milly's horse, a pretty palomino mare that looked as if it would be able to keep up with Duke.

"Everything about ready?" Clint asked a little warily.

"Sure is," Milly said. "Ben here has agreed to live out at my ranch. He's going to watch over the place while I'm gone."

"You are?"

Ben smiled. "That's right."

"What about this livery?" Clint asked.

"I can ride in every day and take care of things and do what shoeing comes my way. It ain't that far out to Milly's ranch."

"Good enough," Clint said, astounded by the sudden change of atmosphere between this pair. When he'd left them an hour ago, they'd been ready to kill each other. Now they were all grins and sunshine.

"Let's ride."

"You mind if Ben comes along as far as the ranch?" Milly asked. "I got some things I need to show him before we leave."

"I didn't know we were going to make any stops," Clint said, managing to hide his irritation. "I thought that you were in some all-fired hurry to find that brother of yours."

"Oh, I am! But Clint, this is important. It won't do any good to retrieve Jackson if the ranch has all gone to hell by the time we return. Why, he'd just take one look at it, rein his horse around, and gallop away. But Ben has agreed to do some repairs while we're gone."

"That's right," Ben said, unable to keep his eyes off Milly. "I'm pretty handy with a hammer, saw, paintbrush, and nails as well as a forge."

"I'm sure you are," Clint said, shaking his head in surprise. "Well, then, let's get your horse saddled and let's ride. If we don't get out of here pretty soon, we might as well just spend another night in Huggins and leave first thing in the morning."

But it took nearly another hour before Ben Bandy was ready to leave. He'd decided to spend the night at Milly's ranch, so he'd needed to feed all his livery horses and make sure they had plenty of water.

"I'd better fix up a sign and put it on the barn door telling folks where I'm off to," Ben said, dismounting just as Clint thought that they were finally ready to go.

Clint gripped his saddle horn with impatience. He looked up at the sky. Hell, it was midafternoon. Figuring at least an hour's delay at Milly's ranch, they wouldn't get ten miles before dark forced them to make camp for the night. Traveling with a woman sure had a way of slowing a man down.

As they rode north, Clint mostly kept quiet as Milly and Ben talked about horses and cattle, the weather, and the state of affairs in West Texas. The sun was still plenty hot, and Clint's mood was sour. He was thinking how much simpler and less bothersome it would have been to be traveling alone. To rise early in the morning when the day was cool and to make twenty-five or thirty miles by midafternoon, then to find some shady place beside a stream and make a quiet, easy camp for himself.

"You're being mighty quiet," Ben said, looking so happy it was positively revolting. "What's the matter?"

"Sometimes quiet is preferable to clacking tongues," Clint grumbled.

Both Milly and Ben raised their eyebrows in surprise and question. "You mad about something?" Milly asked.

"Nope. How much farther is this ranch of yours?" Clint asked, irritated because they had been angling more to the east than the west the past few miles, which meant that they were traveling in the wrong direction.

"Not more than five more miles."

"And you're going to ride into Huggins every day and back?" Clint asked.

"Sure," Ben said. " 'Course, I'll need to get an early start."

"Damned early," Clint growled.

When at last they topped a rise of land and came into sight of the Lane ranch, it was almost sundown, and Clint was anything but impressed. The ranch house was shaded by a circle of huge cottonwood trees, but they couldn't hide the fact that the place was in sorry repair. The house was little more than a ramshackle cabin, half rock, half logs. The barns, if a man could call them barns, were sagging, and most of them had big holes in their roofs. There was a water well in the ranch yard, but the little roof that shielded the well was falling down.

Clint saw no horses, no cattle, no cow, and not even a dog. The only living things on the place were a flock of skinny chickens that came running out cackling as if they were starved, which they probably were.

"Well," Milly said, "what do you think?"

"It's quite a place," Clint said at last.

Milly frowned. "Is that all you got to say? Why, I realize that it ain't very fancy, but we've got enough land to make it pay handsomely. Problem is, it just needs a little shine."

"It needs that," Ben said, expelling a long sigh. "It needs a whole lot of shine."

"Aw," Milly said, trying to force enthusiasm into her voice, "Ben, a man with your energy and talent will have this place fixed up in no time at all. Why, by the time we return with Jackson, it'll be a showplace."

"Well, now, I wouldn't go that far," Ben said, dismounting as the chickens gathered around them.

"Tie your horses at the rail and come on inside," Milly said cheerfully. "Clint, it's up to you, but it doesn't seem to make much sense in pushing on tonight, does it?"

"Nope. Be dark in another hour."

"Good!" Milly whacked the dust from her pants with her riding gloves. "You boys take care of the horses. Water in the well is low, but it'll seep up three or four buckets. I'm afraid we're fresh out of hay in the barn, but I think there's a sack of grain out there someplace. When you finish feeding the horses, toss a little to those damned noisy chickens. And see if they've laid any eggs."

"Where would they be?"

"Oh, probably in the barn or out around in the grass somewheres," Milly said. "And if they still aren't laying, catch up one or two and pluck 'em for the pot."

Clint and Ben exchanged glances. Neither of them had expected anything like these hard times. When they walked away, Clint whispered, "If Art Bacon had seen this place he'd cheated Milly's father out of, he might have given it back."

"Yeah," Ben said, "only it's the land that's worth something. Last time I was out here this place looked real fine. That was when old Pete was sober and took pride in the place. But that also was a damned lot of whiskey ago."

"Yeah," Clint said. "I can see that."

He and Ben had to crank the bucket up and down the well for nearly twenty minutes to get enough water for their thirsty horses. After that, they fed them some moldy grain from a mouse-eaten sack and tossed a few handfuls to the chickens.

Glancing back toward the house, Clint said, "Tell me something, Ben. How did you and Milly bury the hatchet so fast back in Huggins? One minute you're ready to cut each other's throats, the next you're acting like sweethearts. What happened?"

"We struck a deal."

"And that was?"

The blacksmith shrugged his big shoulders. "Milly brought it up. She said that if Jackson wouldn't or couldn't return to help her—or even if he did but wouldn't stay—then if I helped her out, she'd let me buy half interest in this place."

"Hmm," Clint mused. "That's interesting. But you must be reconsidering the offer right now after looking around."

"Nope," Ben said. "I'd stick and fix things up even if there wasn't anything left standing at all. Why? Because it'd keep me close to Milly and, in time, she'd marry me."

"I see." Clint smiled. "Well, maybe you've got it pegged right. I know how you feel about that girl."

"Of course you do," Ben said, stepping up close to the Gunsmith and pinning him with a penetrating look, " 'cause I told you. But what I don't know is how *you* feel about her."

Clint shifted uncomfortably. Ben Bandy was looking pretty damned threatening. "I like her," he hedged, "but I'm too much like Jackson. I could never be tied down to a place like this. I'd go crazy out here working sunup to sundown."

"You sure?"

"Dead sure."

Bandy relaxed. "Good! I'm not worried about Jackson being the fly in the ointment. It was you that had me concerned. I thought you might go sweet on Milly and decide to take a try at rebuilding this ranch. That would leave us enemies."

"You have absolutely nothing to fear," Clint vowed.

Ben Bandy's square face split into a wide grin. He grabbed the Gunsmith's hand and pumped it up and down. "Just one thing," he said. "I plan to marry that girl, so I'd take it real unkind if you . . . well, you know. If you compromised her virginity. If you was to do that, I'd have to kill you or you'd have to kill me. That'd be all there was to it."

Clint swallowed. He felt sweat pop out on his forehead. He'd thought he would be sleeping in the old ranch house with Milly tonight, but now he realized what a monumental mistake that would have been.

"Nothing to worry about," he said with a weak laugh. "She's as safe with me as she would be with her own brother."

"Better be a whole lot safer," Ben said grimly. "I wouldn't trust one of my mares to that sonofabitch Jackson Lane. He'll mount anything."

"Oh." Clint pried his hand loose with no small amount of difficulty. "I guess we'd better go egg hunting, huh?"

"To hell with eggs," Bandy growled, picking up a broken board that had fallen off the roof of the barn. "Let's go kill us some damn chickens."

Clint nodded. He sure hoped that Milly wasn't expecting him to spend the night in her bed, either. One false word and all hell was going to break loose.

Ben Bandy was a man in love, and Lord help the poor sonofabitch who aroused his jealousy.

EIGHT

After their chicken dinner, Clint arose from the table and forced a yawn. "I'm mighty tired tonight. Think I'll bed down in the livery and get some extra shut-eye."

Instant protest formed on Milly's lips, but before she could utter a word of objection, Ben Bandy said, "Yeah, good idea, Clint. Me and Milly need to go over what needs to be done here while you're gone. That will take a little while. Right?"

"Uh . . . right," Milly said, not sounding a bit pleased with this sudden shift of arrangements.

Clint left the rundown old house and wearily plodded out to the barn. In truth, his side was paining him a little, and he was weary. Besides, he was determined that he and Milly would get an early start tomorrow morning. This Texas heat was withering him away, and he could hardly wait to get to higher, cooler country.

Clint checked on Duke once and then spread his bedroll out in the empty barn and stared up at the stars that were plainly visible through the decrepit roof, with about half its shingles missing.

This place was a disaster, and if poor Ben was willing to half-kill himself to win Milly's undying affection and hand in marriage, then more power to him. He'd deserve everything he got—the girl and the ranch.

Clint listened to the murmur of their conversation from the house. Up in the rafters over his head, the chickens stirred fitfully, and he shifted his blankets aside so he would not be covered with chicken shit come daybreak.

A tired smile softened the Gunsmith's ruggedly handsome features. Perhaps big Ben would end up in Milly Lane's bed tonight himself. If so, that was fine. Clint was not a jealous man, and although he had thoroughly enjoyed making love to Milly the night before, he knew that it was Ben, rather than himself, who was best suited to Milly's long-term happiness.

He slept wonderfully well that night, and when the rooster high over his head began to crow, the Gunsmith sat up and knuckled his eyes. Beside him, Ben lay covered with a blanket drenched in chicken shit. Clint almost laughed out loud. That served the big blacksmith right for staying up late and then creeping into the barn in the darkness.

Clint rolled to his feet, pulled on his pants and boots, then buckled on his gunbelt before he grabbed his shirt and ambled outside just in time to watch a beautiful sunrise seep liquid gold across the flat countryside. The air was still cool and invigorating, and when Clint drew a bucket of water up from the poor well, it even tasted sweet.

He drank his fill, washed the sleep from his eyes, and then carried the leaking bucket over to water Duke. It took him another twenty minutes or so before he finished watering the horses, and by then Ben came lumbering out, disgustedly wiping chicken droppings from his arm.

"Latest I've slept in years," he muttered. "Goddamn chickens! They come down from those rafters, I'm going to wring their necks."

Clint grinned. "Maybe you didn't get to bed very early. Anyway, I don't envy you your job here. This place is going to be a man-killer to fix up."

"It won't be that bad. Couple of months of hard work."

"Months?" Clint asked with skepticism. "How about years?"

"Naw." Ben wiped his chicken-soiled arm clean on his pants leg. He stretched his muscular frame and yawned. "I finally got up enough nerve to ask Milly to marry me last night."

"You did. Well, congratulations!"

"She turned me down cold," Ben said between clenched teeth.

Clint's smile crumbled. "Oh. Well, I'm sorry. But you know how women are. They say one thing today, another thing tomorrow. She'll change her mind."

"I don't know," Ben said, his voice taking on a hostile edge. "Milly says she's torn between lovin' the both of us. That's right," Ben continued, jaw jutting out and his fists knotting at his sides. "I thought you were on my side, and now this."

Clint raised both of his hands in a gesture of pure innocence. "Now, wait just a minute here, partner. I can't help it if Milly has got things a little confused. I don't love her, and as soon as I help her find her brother, I'm going to light out for the high country and never see her again."

"She know that?"

"She sure does."

"Well, just make sure you keep tellin' her the facts of the matter and keep your hands off of her. Understand me?"

Clint was about to say something about how he did not like to be threatened when Ben poked him in the chest with a thick forefinger to emphasize his point.

"That's it," Clint hissed, knotting his own knuckles and winging an uppercut from his boottops.

His fist slammed up against Ben's gut and bounced off just as if he'd struck a Cheyenne buffalo hide shield.

"Uh-oh," Clint muttered, taking a step back and then ducking a big overhand right that moved a lot of still air.

Clint tried the man's chin. He landed a left jab and followed it with a right cross. Ben staggered, but other than blinking a couple of times, he showed no effect of the punches. The Gunsmith knew he was in deep trouble.

"Now, listen," Clint said, backing up as the man came wading in at him, "I think we ought to talk this out. There's room for some understanding here and—"

Clint swallowed his words as he ducked another round-house punch. He chopped Ben across the cheek and opened it up to the bone. Ben shook his head like a bull and kept coming.

For the next few seconds, Clint was doing everything he could to keep from being battered senseless. Ben was slow, but when his fists struck the Gunsmith's upraised arms, it felt as if he were being battered by a tree limb.

"Enough, damnit!" Clint shouted.

"Come on and fight! We'll show Milly who's the best man."

Clint sighed. He knew full well that he could not match the man's strength, and to hit him in the head would raise more of a risk to his hands than to Ben's jaw.

Clint took a thundering blow to the side of the head, and he staggered backward as Ben charged. The man grabbed him around the body and crushed him in a bear hug that would have broken a whiskey barrel.

"Let go of me!" Clint grunted. "You big fool, what's the matter with you?"

But Ben wouldn't let go, so Clint drove his boot heel down the man's shin. Ben cried out in pain, and when the pressure of his hold eased, Clint pulled an arm free and battered the man in the nose repeatedly until it broke and Ben howled with pain.

"Enough!" Clint panted, breaking free.

"Not until I whip you into the ground and show Milly I'm the better man!"

"That doesn't prove anything, you big fool!"

But Ben must have disagreed, because he lowered his head and charged with arms outstretched to gather Clint in and break him in two.

The Gunsmith did what he should have done from the start. He yanked his Colt and used its heavy barrel to put a new, permanent part in the big man's hair.

Ben dropped like a lung-shot buffalo. He kicked a few times and then lay still. Clint knelt by his side and examined the laceration in the man's scalp.

"I sure hated to do that," he mumbled, "but you went crazy on me. Best thing you can do right now is to sleep until I'm out of here."

"Clint! Ben!" Milly cried, hurrying out of the ranch house. "What happened?"

Clint holstered his gun. "I put him back to sleep for a few hours."

"But—"

"Milly, get your things packed while I get the horses ready. We're pulling out of here before he wakes up."

She bit her lower lip. "Did he fight over me?"

"It sure wasn't over a chicken," Clint snapped. "Of course it was over you! The man is crazy for you, Milly. He's not in his right mind and, if you ever decided to marry him, you'd better make sure you never cause him any jealousy."

Milly swallowed and knelt beside Ben. She touched his bleeding scalp and looked up at Clint, anger in her eyes. "Did you have to pistol-whip him like that?"

"Yes," Clint said, "or he'd have beaten me to a pulp. Now come on and get ready. If he wakes up again, I might have to kill him."

The threat worked, and it sent Milly scurrying into the house. Clint wasted no time going into the barn and getting the horses saddled.

Fifteen minutes later, he and Milly were ready to go.

"We can't just leave him lying unconscious in the yard like that!"

"What else can we do?" Clint asked, rubbing his jaw and feeling around inside his mouth with his tongue, counting a few loose molars.

"You go on ahead. I'll stay with him until he wakes up, and then I'll follow."

"I won't wait," Clint vowed. "I said I'd help you find your brother, though I don't know why I made such a foolish promise. But I mean to get out of this country as soon as I can. You can come or stay, it doesn't matter to me."

She looked hurt. "Do you mean that?"

Clint softened. "Listen," he said, "I just don't want to have to shoot that big blacksmith when he wakes up. So stay if you want, but then come along and make sure that he doesn't follow with blood in his eye."

"I will," Milly promised. "I'll be right along."

"All right." Clint took the lead rope to their pack horse and mounted Duke. "You see those low, distant mountains?"

She was cradling Ben's cracked skull when she looked up to follow where he was pointing.

"Yes."

"That's in line with Colorado and where I'll be heading. I mean to camp in those hills tonight."

"I'll overtake you long before then."

"See that you do," he growled as he touched spurs to Duke's flanks and rode off at a gallop.

When Clint was still a speck on the flat Texas horizon, Milly laid Ben's head down and went to her well. She drew a bucketful of water and carried it to the unconscious blacksmith, then carefully poured it over his head.

Ben awoke, sputtering. Milly dropped the bucket and knelt by his side.

"It's all right, darling. He's gone."

Ben was still dazed. "He is? Where?"

"He's going to Colorado. I'm going to catch up with him."

"Don't," Ben pleaded. "Stay with me, Milly. Jackson won't come back, and even if he did, he'd be worse than useless."

"He's my brother," Milly said. "After he started drinking, Pa drove him too hard. Made him wild and crazy and a drinker like his father. I owe it to Jackson to ask him back. Half this ranch is his, too."

"He'd only want to sell his half," Ben said. "He'd just want the money, and then he'd gamble it away."

"I know that's what he'd have done the last time I saw him, but maybe not anymore. I got to give him the chance, Ben. I owe him. I'd never forgive myself if I didn't try to find and offer him a helping hand."

Ben sighed. "Okay," he said, "but what about the Gunsmith?"

"No promises," she said. "I just don't know yet."

"But you do love me?"

Milly nodded and unbuttoned her blouse. She took his rough and calloused hand and placed it on her bare breast. She sighed and closed her eyes.

"I guess this shows how much I think of you, doesn't it?"

He swallowed noisily. "It sure does. Can I feel the other one, too?"

"Sure, Ben."

He smiled and reached up to cradle both of her breasts. A look a joy and peace touched his battered face.

"Oh, Milly," he said, voice near choking, "I'd give my life for you."

"I know that," she whispered, moving her chest back and forth across his hands and loving the feel of it. "And I'll be back as soon as I can."

"You won't recognize this place," he promised. "I swear you won't."

"I know."

Milly gently removed his hands from her breasts and then buttoned her blouse. She bent and kissed the blacksmith on the lips, and before he could enfold her in his powerful arms, she stood up and went to her horse.

" 'Bye, Ben. You don't work yourself too awful hard out here, and you eat right. Hear me?"

He managed a nod.

"I love you, Ben."

He nodded again and then watched as the girl blew him a kiss and then galloped north into the soft, shimmering heat waves.

NINE

The Gunsmith and Milly reached the Canadian River a week later, and the weather had suddenly turned cool.

"We'll rest a full day here," Clint said, noting how the outlines of Duke's ribs were plainly showing once again.

"You won't hear any arguments from me," Milly said, looking at the dark thunderheads approaching from the north.

Clint hobbled Duke and then unbridled the gelding before he worked loose his latigo and unsaddled. The gelding began to eat as if it were half-starved, and the Gunsmith took care of their packhorse and Milly's horse next.

Lugging two saddles under the trees, Clint said, "The horses badly need to graze on this riverside grass. They could also use some rest, and from the looks of those big thunderheads we could be facing a pretty good storm. You don't want to be out there in the open in the thunder and lightning."

"I can feel the wind picking up," Milly said, looking up at the cottonwood leaves that were beginning to shiver.

Milly hobbled her palomino and helped carry her saddle over beside his own. "Did you bring a rain slicker?"

Milly shook her head.

"Then you can use mine."

"Are you going to light a fire so I can heat some food and coffee?"

"Unless we can find some good shelter, there's not much point in it," Clint said, squatting down and waiting for the storm.

Milly sat down beside him. "Think we might be in for a tornado?"

"Nope." Clint pulled his Stetson down tighter. "Most tornadoes stay a little to the north and east of us. I think what we've got coming is nothing more nor less than a damn good storm."

They both leaned back against the same thick cottonwood and watched as the thunderheads and a wall of dark clouds rolled in at them. At the end of another hour, the wind picked up dramatically, and the boughs of the trees began to bend and dance.

"We can't allow the horses to graze any longer," Clint said, coming to his feet and grabbing ropes.

Milly pushed out into the wind, too, and they caught the horses and led them, still hobbled, into the trees. Clint tied the three animals securely and then began an earnest search for a place where they would be as protected as possible from the elements.

As luck would have it, they found an ideal hideout under a huge fallen tree. "Looks like we're not the first to seek shelter. There's even a fire ring for us, Milly."

Before the girl slipped under the tree, Clint put his weight and muscle against the trunk, and when he was sure it wasn't going to shift, said, "Go ahead, get the packs and I'll drag the saddles under here, too. It's going to be a little cramped, but at least we don't have to worry about lightning knocking a tree on us."

Clint and Milly wasted no time dragging their saddles, gear, and supplies under shelter, and by the time they scooted into the depression under the tree, it was starting to rain.

"Listen to that thunder and lightning," Clint said, keeping an eye on their nervous horses.

Milly reached into her coat pocket and fumbled for matches. She stared at them a moment, and Clint just shook his head. It would be both useless and dangerous to try to start a fire with the swirling wind and rain.

A huge roll of thunder was followed by a searing bolt of lightning that ripped down through the dark sky and struck a cottonwood tree somewhere upriver.

All three horses reared back on their haunches and struggled to tear free, but their ropes held, and Clint was at their sides a moment later, soothing their fears.

When he looked over at the river, he saw that it had risen at least five feet.

"Milly!" he shouted into the wind.

Somehow she heard him and came running. Clint shouted again, "We need to find a tree up higher and away from this river! It's coming up too fast!"

She nodded, and Clint handed her the rope to her palomino. Struggling and slipping on the wet carpet of leaves and trying to see through a cold, pelting rain, they moved the horses to higher ground, and Clint personally tied all three from overhead limbs so they could not get their heads down and pull with the full force of their body.

"Nothing else we can do now!" Clint shouted, grabbing Milly and hurrying back toward their little shelter.

Clint pushed Milly in, and just as he was about to follow, he heard something strange.

"What is it?" Milly shouted.

Clint straightened and peered into the fading light and the downpour. Overhead the wind was almost shrieking, and yet . . . "There, I heard it again!"

"What?"

"Someone yelling for help," Clint said, "from the direction of the river."

Clint charged down toward the river and squinted out at the brown, roiling waters. Suddenly he saw two men just upriver hanging onto a log. They both looked to be in danger of being swept under.

"Damn!" Clint shouted, turning and racing for his saddle and rope.

Very quickly the Gunsmith explained what he had just seen. "If I don't give them a hand, they'll drown for sure."

"Let me help."

Clint nodded. He and Milly set off for the river, battling the wind and the squalling rain.

"Hang on!" Clint shouted when he was as close as he dared get to the men.

Pitching a loop, he saw the two men reach for it and then began to fight to see which one could get it around his shoulders.

"Nearer man first!" Clint raged. "Damnit, nearer man first!"

He was not sure if they heard him, but the nearer man seemed to win the argument. He got Clint's loop over his shoulders and then managed to drag himself over the log.

"Dig in your heels and pull!" Clint yelled back over his shoulder to Milly.

The man was large, and when he hit the end of the rope, the current almost dragged them all into the Canadian. For a minute Clint thought he and Milly were going to have to release the rope and let go, but the man suddenly got his footing. Between the two of them, they managed to pull the bedraggled man to safety.

"Man, am I glad to see you!" the stranger roared. He was shirtless and covered with mud. His torso was badly scratched and his black hair was plastered wetly against his skull.

"Get that rope off and help us pull in your friend," Clint ordered.

The man did as he was told, and it took the Gunsmith three attempts to hurl a second loop far enough to reach the other man.

"All right, let's go!" Clint roared as lightning struck the

top of a tall tree and made it smoke and blaze.

Clint and Milly pulled with all their might as the second man released his grip on the tree trunk and went thrashing downriver.

With the three of them, they had an easier time hauling in the second man. He was also tall, but slender and shivering, as if he had the ague.

"We found a little shelter under a fallen log!" Clint shouted, motioning for the men to follow him.

When they reached the log, the shivering man didn't wait for an invitation but ducked inside. His partner followed.

"Now, wait a minute!" Clint yelled down at the two mud-streaked men. "We got a young lady here and—"

"No," Milly objected. "They look awful."

"But—"

Milly took Clint's arm and led him a few feet down toward the roots of the log. "We can squeeze in under here. Maybe burrow out a little dirt, bark, and some leaves, and get under."

Clint supposed she was right, but it rankled him the way the two men had just taken over their shelter. "You notice they didn't even bother to say thanks for our saving their lives?"

"I noticed," Milly said. "I wonder what happened."

"Must have been a flash flood," Clint said, dropping to his knees and furiously scooping out a hollow under the log. "They probably camped right next to the water somewhere within a couple of miles. Got washed away when the water hit them."

"Here," she said, bumping him, "let me do some of the work."

Clint eased back on his haunches, and when he tipped his head back to stare up at the dark, boiling sky, a sheet of water cascaded off the brim of his hat and ran down his back.

"That ought to do it," Milly said, wiggling under the tree. "Come on!"

Clint removed his hat. He was already soaking wet, but at

least he might be able to avoid catching a chill if he could get out of the cold wind.

As soon as he was dug in beside Milly, she put her arms around his neck and they lay side by side, staring out at the pouring rain. An especially brilliant bolt of lightning caused Milly to start, and Clint hugged her tight. He slipped his hand under her shirt and up to cover her cold, wet breast.

"This might not be such a bad deal after all," he said, feeling a warm glow creep up from his loins.

But Milly surprised him when she said, "Don't be ridiculous. There's not enough room even if we wanted to."

"I want to," Clint said.

"Well," she replied, "I'm afraid I don't."

Clint removed his hand from under her shirt. "You don't?"

"No."

"Mind telling me why not? Last time you couldn't seem to get your fill of me."

"That was different," she said. "I was in Huggins then."

"So?"

"So now we're in the middle of a terrible storm, I'm wet and cold, and there are two not very friendly men less than ten feet away from us. Don't you see how all those things might make a difference?"

"Yeah, I guess," Clint said, trying to hide his annoyance. "But if a western man and a woman always held off making love for a feather bed, candles, and lace curtains, the Indians would never have had a thing to worry about."

Clint kissed her mouth. "I just thought, since we can't light a fire, we might generate a little heat with friction."

She laughed. "You are a smooth-talkin' man, aren't you."

Clint gave up. "So what are we supposed to do until the storm is over to pass the time?"

"We could talk."

"All right." Clint rolled over onto his back but kept one eye on the horses, who were still dancing around at the end of their tethers. "Talk."

"You talk," she said. "Have you ever been married?"

"Nope. Come close a time or two."

When he didn't say anything more, Milly prodded, "So what happened?"

The Gunsmith frowned. "Oh, I dunno. Either they got tired of me or I got tired of them. Not too many women think a lawman is a good long-term prospect."

"But you're not a lawman anymore."

"No," he said, "I'm not. But there are plenty of men out West whose paths I've crossed. A good lot of them would just love to sort of pay me back for one thing or another. There are more than a couple of women who wouldn't think twice about sticking a knife in my belly, either."

"I see." Milly frowned. "Yes, given that, I can understand why some women would shy away from wanting to marry you."

"Exactly, and those that don't look at marriage as a long-term arrangement aren't the kind that attract me."

"Do I attract you?"

"Of course."

Milly frowned. She brushed a little mud from his cheek. "You attract the hell out of me, too."

He started to slip his hand back under her shirt. "Well, then?"

"No," she said, shoving his hand away. "Not unless you change your attitude about marriage."

It was the Gunsmith's turn to laugh, but there wasn't much humor in it. "I see. So that's it. Marriage or no play."

Milly's eyes sparked even in the dim light. "Ben Bandy would marry me even if I was poor and ugly."

"Poor," Clint said agreeably, "but not ugly."

"Well . . . well, he was willing to work like a dog this summer for me, and all I had to do was to let him touch me here."

Milly touched the places where her wet shirt was plastered to her firm breasts. "It was enough for him."

"Then I guess that really does prove he has a true love for you, Milly. A man that would settle for just a touch is a rare man."

"Oh, he wanted a lot more," she said quickly. "You men always do. But Ben is gentleman enough to respect a lady when she says no."

Clint could feel his anger starting to rise. He grabbed the girl in his arms, twisted her body under his own, and then he said, "Well, I'm cold and I'm no gentleman this hard afternoon, Milly. And last week in Huggins, you didn't act like a lady. So let's stop pretending."

Clint kissed her mouth, and his hand unbuttoned her shirt. She struggled a moment and then wrapped her arms around his neck and kissed him passionately.

"Damn you, Clint!" she said with a smile. "I'm never going to get you to marry me, am I."

"Nope," he said as he began to remove her riding skirt.

"This is a terrible place to make love."

"You do it whenever and wherever you can," he said, squeezing his backbone up against the underside of the log and trying to get his own pants unbuttoned.

A few clumsy minutes later, Clint was mounted again and as the storm raged and their horses threw their heads about in fear, Clint made the most of the situation, and by the time he and Milly were finished, the storm was passing and they weren't cold anymore.

"Well, would you look at them!" a voice boomed. "He's humping her under the same damn log we were under!"

Clint and Milly looked up to see the two men they'd saved from the river staring at them with big grins. They were wearing the two extra shirts that Clint had packed for the trip, and if that didn't anger him enough, one man had his extra Colt in his fist and the other had his Winchester.

Clint was painfully aware of his awful predicament. He was helpless, really, but he tried to bluff. "You boys better put those weapons back where you found them and get away from here real quick or you're in deep, deep trouble."

The bigger of the pair levered a cartridge into the Gunsmith's own rifle. He pointed the weapon right at Clint's head and growled, "Is that right?"

Clint's hand strayed down his side, vainly groping for his own six-gun, which was stuffed somewhere back under the log. The Gunsmith could feel Milly's heart pounding again, just as it had when they made love.

"You want me to blow your damned head off with you layin' on her, or would you rather come out from under there and save that little girl from seein' a real ugly thing?"

"I'll come out," Clint said, feeling Milly pressing his gun into his left hand. Clint was right-handed, but there would be no chance to switch hands without it being seen by the two strangers.

"Then come along!" the slender man cackled. "I can't wait to take your damned place on her."

Clint extended his Colt back as far as he could before he thumbed back the hammer. Accurately shooting upward with his off hand was going to be almost impossible. And yet he could not afford to miss, because Milly's life would be in almost as much jeopardy as his own in any ensuing gun battle.

I'll go for the big man first because he's closer and the larger target, Clint thought, edging the Colt forward along his side.

"Come on!" the smaller man with the pistol hissed, reaching down for Clint's arm to drag him out.

In that instant, the larger of the two was blocked from view, and Clint changed his plan. As the smaller man leaned forward and grabbed his right wrist, Clint jammed his Colt forward and pulled the trigger.

The man's face exploded in a shower of crimson. Clint heard Milly scream, and then the man dropped before them.

"Goddamn you!" the bigger man shouted, flinging up the Winchester and firing downward.

The bullet ate bark, which tore into Clint's shoulder and neck. Clint triggered off a pair of reckless shots as he tried to shield Milly's face.

He heard a roar of pain and then the sound of boots sucking mud. "He's running away!"

Clint had to shove the dead man's body away from the trunk of the tree so he could drag himself free. Switching his gun to his right hand, he started to run, but his pants were down around his knees and he went down in the mud, cussing and reaching for his pants. When he had them up, he scrambled to his feet and went after the big man with the rifle.

"Stop!" Clint shouted.

The big man was hobbling, bent over at the waist and in great pain. When he heard Clint's voice, he spun around, threw the rifle to his shoulder, and took a bullet through the chest for all his trouble.

The man staggered backward. The Winchester sagged in his arms and Clint shouted, "Drop it!"

The fool wagged his head. Struggling as if he were lifting the back of a wagon instead of a rifle, Clint watched as the man slowly retreated toward the river. When he reached the banks of the Canadian, he just kept backing up.

"You leave me alone!" he shouted.

"Throw the rifle up on the bank!"

But again the man wagged his head, and this time he managed to get the Winchester levered and all the way up to his shoulder.

Clint shot him twice more, each of his bullets sending the fool deeper into the water until he sat down, then rolled face over. The strong, muddy current grabbed his body, and he began to bob his way downriver. Clint dropped his gun and rushed into the water. Bending way over, he groped along the cold, murky river bottom, but his rifle was gone, torn away by the current.

The Gunsmith slogged back to shore and saw that the body was already sweeping around a sharp bend in the river. Then it disappeared.

Clint shook his head. Things like this were enough to sour a man on ever again helping someone in desperate trouble.

He would miss that rifle very much on the long trail north into Colorado.

TEN

The first thing Clint did when they rode up Denver's busy Larimer Street was rein his horse before the sheriff's office.

"Oh, Clint," Milly sighed, "can't we at least find a room to clean up in first?"

"I'd rather take a couple of minutes here first," Clint said, taking the reins out of Milly's hand and tying them to the hitching post, then tying their packhorse between. "Come along now."

"But I'm sure a sight!"

Clint rubbed the thick stubble on his jaw. "I'm not going to be mistaken for any prominent official, either. But we need to find out if anyone has seen your brother in these parts. Depending on what answer we hear inside, we can figure our next step."

Milly didn't like that, but she clamped her jaw in silence as she dismounted. She also fumbled around in her saddlebags for her purse. Inside was a daguerreotype of Jackson Lane. It was at least five years old, but Milly was sure her brother's appearance hadn't greatly changed.

Clint offered Milly his arm as he escorted her up to the sheriff's door and opened it.

"Afternoon," the sheriff called, "come on inside."

Clint followed Milly in, and even though he had to admit that she looked dirty and bedraggled after their long, hard trip up from Texas, she still had the ability to attract plenty of attention.

The sheriff was in his fifties, medium-sized with a watermelon belly and the red-veined nose of a man who drank too much whiskey. Beside him was a much younger man, and when Clint saw the badge on his chest, he knew that this was the deputy who probably did most of the real law work in Denver.

"My name is Sheriff Stanley Yates, and this is Deputy Otis Holland. What can we help you folks out with today?"

Clint introduced Milly and then himself.

"*You're* the Gunsmith?" the deputy blurted. "Why, you look like a common trailhand to me."

"He's got a great way with words, doesn't he," Clint said sarcastically to the sheriff.

Holland didn't even hear him. The young fool had immediately dismissed Clint and was already absorbed by Milly's presence.

Yates dropped his boots down from his desktop to the floor with a loud thump. He came around to shake Clint's hand. "I've heard a great deal 'bout you, Mr. Adams. All of it good. Welcome to Denver. My office stands ready to help you and Miss Lane however we can."

"Good," Clint said. Very quickly he told the sheriff about the need to locate Jackson Lane. He finished by saying, "Milly, show him that picture you carry."

Milly produced the daguerreotype, and the sheriff stared at it for several seconds before he smiled and said, "Sure, I know Jackson pretty well. Every saloon owner in this town knows him even better."

"He's still a drinker, is he?" Milly asked with disapproval written all over her pretty face.

"You bet he is! Gets drunk every Saturday night and raises hell all over town. Best chance of finding him is right here in my jail come Sunday morning. Isn't that right, Otis?"

"Sure is." Otis clucked his tongue. "That brother of yours, Miss Lane, he's a ringtailed badger. Tough as they come and wild as a river. Unless he's pretty much gone, I won't mess with him. Even drunk, he's dangerous to handle."

"I'm sure that you won't ever have to 'handle' him again, Deputy," Clint said. "The purpose of our visit is to bring Jackson back to his home near Huggins, Texas."

"Be no loss to Colorado if he went," the deputy said. "A lot of saloon owners and women in this town would breathe a mite easier."

"You've got a way of using your mouth before your brain," Clint said. "If I were you, I'd work on that."

Now the deputy heard the insult in Clint's voice, and he wasn't pleased. "I guess you think you're a real big deal because you once wore a badge and probably shot some famous outlaw in the back when he was takin' a piss out in the alley. Well—"

Clint's fist made a short arc that terminated at the point of the man's jaw. The deputy crashed over his own chair, lit on his backside, and slid all the way to cell bars.

Clint turned on the sheriff. "I'd fire him before he gets himself or someone else shot."

Yates rubbed his own jaw. "I'll think on that some, Gunsmith. But until I do, he's still my deputy and I won't have anyone—even you—assaulting him. You do it again, you're going to jail and then before a judge. We got a tough judge in Denver, and your reputation won't cut any ice with him. Savvy?"

"Yeah," Clint said. "I'll keep that warning well in mind."

"See that you do, then," the sheriff said. "And if you can't find Jackson Lane before Sunday, stop by and most likely you'll find him behind those bars."

"It's Friday," Milly said. "Where is my brother working?"

"Working? I don't think he does work. Not steady, at least. Mostly you'll find him breaking horses at some ranch around these parts."

The sheriff turned to look at his deputy, who was rubbing his jaw and pulling himself to his feet. "Otis, do you know where Jackson is working right now?"

"Last I heard he was going mustang-hunting somewhere up north. 'Course, you know how he was always going to go mustanging. Hell, the only thing he really hunted was women and the bottle."

Clint took a threatening step toward the deputy, but Milly grabbed his arm. "Please," she begged, "getting yourself arrested and sentenced to jail time won't help me find Jackson. I need you, Clint. Just leave him be."

Clint pointed a finger at sheriff and said, "You really better fire him pronto, Yates. A man like that can make this office more enemies than you can handle."

"I'll put some thought to it," the sheriff said. "Now get along. Miss Lane is right about getting yourself arrested if you touch my deputy again."

Clint allowed Milly to take his arm and pull him out the door. Clint untied the horses and mounted Duke. "In the towns I sheriffed in," he said, "a deputy like that wouldn't stay alive a week before someone shot him dead. I can't understand why a sheriff would hire a mouthy kid like that."

"Maybe he's his son-in-law or something."

"Yeah," Clint said, "that must be the reason."

"Can we get a room now?"

"Sure," Clint said. "We'll have bath and—"

"And get some new, clean clothes," Milly said. "In fact, I don't see much point in having a bath until we have clean clothes to wear. Do you?"

"Not unless we wear 'em in the tub and skin two cats with the same bar of soap."

Milly laughed because she knew that he was teasing her. They remounted and headed down the street, looking for a well-kept livery where their underfed and overworked horses could recuperate.

That afternoon, they went shopping. Clint had plenty of money from what he'd won from Art Bacon, and he wasn't the kind to save it for his retirement. He bought himself a new black suit, white shirt, and black string tie. He purchased new underwear and stockings. He even bought a new Stetson and would have bought a new pair of boots except that the bootmaker wanted too much money and time.

After an hour of fussing around inside a ladies' store, Milly emerged on the boardwalk with an armful of boxes. A new dress, new hat, new riding habit, and a couple of practical things for the trail back to Texas. She also, Clint was very sure, bought quite a few fresh undergarments.

"I checked, and the Hotel Granite is the best around," Clint said, leading the way. "I even registered us."

"As husband and wife, I hope."

"Sure. I just hope that wild brother of yours isn't as jealous as Ben Bandy was."

"Hell," Milly snorted, "my brother cares nothing for tradition or convention. He wouldn't even wonder about us."

"Good."

Clint helped Milly carry the boxes down to the hotel, which was quite elegant, with a marble-floored lobby and a big crystal chandelier hanging from a domed ceiling.

"It's beautiful," Milly said under her breath. "I've never stayed anywhere so fancy."

"You go back to that ranch, you might never again," Clint said.

"Are you offering me something better?" Milly asked.

"Nope, just pointing out a fact of life."

Milly smiled and headed for the stairs.

"Baths," Clint said, passing the hotel desk clerk. "Bring on lots of hot water."

Several of the other hotel guests turned to stare at Clint and Milly. They were older people, well dressed and well groomed. By their sour expressions, Clint could see that they were not impressed by him and his "wife," but he did not give a damn. When he and Milly got themselves cleaned and dressed up in their new clothes, they'd outshine the lot of them.

Easily.

"Very well, Mr. Adams," the desk clerk said with a bow.

Clint headed up the stairs, watching Milly's cute little behind wag. Hell, he thought, maybe he could show Milly how much fun it was to make love in a hot bathtub.

ELEVEN

"So," Clint said the next morning, "we might as well get dressed, eat some breakfast, and then see if we can find out if your brother is still in town."

Milly groaned. "If you had let me go to sleep last night, I wouldn't be so tired this morning."

Clint grinned, and patted Milly on the butt before he climbed out of bed. "If you want to go back to sleep, then help yourself. I'll eat and then ask questions. If Jackson is still working in these parts, I'll find him. It's one of the things I'm particularly good at."

She smiled lazily and winked. "So far, making love is the thing you're best at as far as I can tell."

Milly climbed out of bed and staggered over to the washbasin. She filled their large porcelain bowl and was anything but ladylike as she splashed water over her face, neck, and upper body.

"What about our bath?"

"You take mine and leave the water. I'll be back in an hour or so."

"You promise you won't do anything without coming to get me first?"

"He's your wayward brother," Clint said. "I'll come get you right away if I get a line on where he's to be found."

This seemed to satisfy Milly. She dried herself, then wobbled back to bed and pulled the covers over herself and was almost instantly asleep.

The Gunsmith smiled. He felt a little tired himself after their late-night session of lovemaking. Sooner or later, he thought, we are going to have to get more sleep and do less messing around. But what the hell, a man could sleep in the grave for all eternity, and it wasn't every night that he slept with a woman as desirable as Milly Lane.

Clint let himself out and was careful to lock the door behind him. He went downstairs and soon found a café to his liking.

"Steak, gravy, biscuits, and eggs. Eggs over easy," he said. "Bring me coffee. Lots of black coffee."

"You got it," the man who waited on him said with a grin.

The coffee came first, but it didn't take long for the steak and the rest to follow. Clint was famished and he ate wolfishly, sopping up the last of the gravy with a biscuit.

"How was it?"

"Is your dinner as good?"

"You bet."

"Then I'll be back," Clint promised, dropping two dollars on the counter. "Keep the change."

"Well, thank you!"

"Say, do you know a man named Jackson Lane? He'd be about twenty-five, sandy-hair and—"

"You sure don't have to describe him for me," the man said. "I know that miserable sonofabitch. I doubt that there is a single saloon, café, or whorehouse in all of Colorado that he hasn't stiffed. I won't serve him anymore unless he pays first."

"That bad?"

"That bad."

"So where is he now?"

"In hell, I hope," the man said before he picked up Clint's dirty dishes. "You want more coffee?"

"Just a little. How would I start out to find him?"

"Go to the whorehouses. Hang out in the worst of our saloons. Go where you wouldn't want to turn your back on the customers. That's your best bet."

"Thanks," Clint said with a frown.

"Look," the man said, pouring coffee, "you're dressed nice. You look like a man with brains and some success in life. Let me offer you a piece of free but very valuable advice: You don't want to find Jackson Lane—you want to avoid him."

"Yeah," Clint said, sipping his coffee, "that's what everyone has been telling me."

"Well then?" the man asked with a shrug of his shoulders. "Listen to them."

Clint would have liked nothing better, but it wasn't in the cards. He'd promised Milly that he'd track down her brother, and a promise was a promise.

He went outside and spied a barbershop. Running his hands through his long, shaggy hair and scratching his beard, he nodded to himself and headed across the street.

"Morning!" the barber called, sizing Clint up as a customer who might give him a good tip for superior service. "Step right up and have a seat."

"Well, what about those fellas over there?" Clint asked, pointing to two men who were smoking cheap cigars and reading old newspapers.

"Aw, they're regulars with nothing better to do than to hang around here so it looks like I'm keeping busy."

"I see," the Gunsmith said, stepping into the barber's chair with the hint of a smile. "Smart business."

"Sure is, except them cigars they smoke are so rank that they chase out a lot of my better customers."

In truth, the cigar smoke was pretty bad, and there was actually a hazy line of it down about three feet from ceiling level.

Clint removed his new black Stetson, and the barber threw his sheet around his neck and drew it tight. "Shave and cut?"

"That's right," Clint said, "and don't scalp me. I'm not looking to put your profession out of business."

"Yes, sir! Just a trim."

The Gunsmith closed his eyes and relaxed as the barber dabbed lather across his jaws and began to stroke his razor against a thick strop.

"You know a man called Jackson Lane?"

"Afraid so."

"Know where I can find him?"

"Cemetery maybe."

Clint's eyes snapped open. "What's that supposed to mean?"

"Just that Lane has a lot of enemies in Denver. I just heard a couple of days ago that there were some men looking for him to pay off some old gambling and other debts he owes."

Clint relaxed. "Well, maybe he's paid them off."

"Not a chance. Lane is the kind that will never pay his debts. He's a welcher. Owes me and every other businessman in Denver. Probably owes a lot of others, too. Men that will kill him if he doesn't settle up."

"The sheriff said that he thought Lane might have gone mustanging up north," Clint said. "That sound reasonable?"

"Not to me."

"Why not?" Clint asked. "From what I hear, Lane is a hell of a horseman."

"Oh, yeah, he's one of the best, so the cowboys say. When he's sober I guess he can ride about anything with hair and legs. He liked to brag that he was better ridin' women than broncs, but if he was, he'd be gettin' it for free instead of payin' the whores."

"So you don't know where is he is?"

"Nope, and I don't want to know."

Clint nodded. He closed his eyes and let the man shave his jowls and cut his hair. The Gunsmith was pretty sure he wasn't going to find anyone in Denver who either liked

Jackson Lane or could really tell him where the man might be found.

Clint said as much to Milly when he went back to his room and rejoined her. Milly, not entirely to his surprise, defended her brother.

"Jackson has a lot of rough edges, but he's got a good heart. I've seen him jump into a fight for no better reason than to help out the underdog."

"From what I hear, he just likes to fight, period. Any excuse will do."

"That's not true!"

"True or not," Clint said, "I'm convinced that we might as well wait until tomorrow morning and then go see if the sheriff has got him locked in jail."

"And if he doesn't?" Milly asked.

"Then we travel north and see if we can catch wind of where he might have gone mustanging."

Milly sighed. "From what you've said so far, it sure sounds like Jackson is unpopular in this town."

"Let's just say that if he were running for public office, he wouldn't have a Chinaman's chance of being elected."

"I'm hungry," Milly said. "So what do we do all day?"

"Eat, sleep, and a couple of other things I think will keep us well occupied."

Milly blushed. "You're awful, Clint."

Clint and Milly finally got their rest and even a good night's sleep. On Sunday morning they dressed early, had breakfast, and headed for the sheriff's office.

"I'm not very optimistic," Milly said.

Clint wasn't either until he opened the door of the sheriff's office and saw that there were at least ten men sleeping off their drunks.

"What the hell you want at this hour?" Deputy Otis Holland snarled.

Clint pushed by the man, dragging Milly behind him. He stopped at the bars and turned to Milly. "You see him?"

The cell was dim and crowded with men stretched all over the floor and two bunks.

"I . . . Jackson! Jackson, is that you?"

One of the men groaned but did not awaken.

"It is him!" Milly cried with joy.

Clint turned to the deputy. "How much to spring him out this morning?"

Holland knuckled his bloodshot eyes. He looked as if he'd had a long, hard night and it was easy to see why by the number of men he'd arrested.

"He busted up the Delta Saloon. Broke a chair over a man's head and sent him to the doctor. Broke a bottle over the bar and hooked someone in the gut, sending him to the doctor. It's a wonder he's still alive. I'd guess he might go to prison this time."

"No!" Milly cried, reaching into her purse. "I'll pay the damages. Every penny."

The deputy fingered a discoloration under his own eye. "He caught me with a good one, too. I'm afraid that I'm not too inclined to let him go."

"How much?" Clint asked roughly.

The deputy's eyes slitted. "I might be convinced to look the other way for . . . oh, fifty dollars."

"Fifty dollars!" Milly cried.

"I told you, he cut up two men and wrecked the saloon. After I pay damages, I won't have much left for myself."

Clint didn't believe a word of it, but he saw no point in arguing. "If you want him to return to Texas, Milly, I'd suggest you pay Holland and let's get your brother out of here, pronto."

Milly tore the money from her purse. "Here," she snapped. "Open the cell."

The deputy took the money and slowly counted it. Clint knew it was more than a month's wages, and yet the man angled for a little more.

"I don't know," Holland complained. "I could lose my job for this. Ain't hardly worth it."

· Clint reached out and snatched the fifty dollars from the deputy's hand. "Then in that case, the hell with it," he said, taking Milly by the arm and turning her toward the door.

"Clint!"

Milly was struggling in protest, but Clint's grip on her arm was firm, and he was propelling her toward the street.

"Now, wait a minute!" Deputy Holland called, rushing up to them before they could get outside. "I didn't say that I wouldn't take the fifty."

Clint spun on the man. "Deputy, you're a disgrace to the law profession. Take the money or leave it, I don't care. Just make up your damned mind!"

"You'd have to promise to get him out of town and not let him come back."

"We'll get him out of town," Clint said, "but we can't promise that he won't return."

"If he does, he'll go to prison. You tell him that."

Clint shoved the deputy so hard that he backpedaled all the way to the cell. "Open it!"

Holland blushed with humiliation, but he did what Clint ordered. He unlocked the cell, grabbed Milly's brother by a boot, and dragged him cussing and sputtering out into the center of his office.

"You get your brother the hell out of this town!"

Clint hurled the money at the man and reached down to grab Jackson Lane. He threw Milly's brother over his shoulder and stomped out the door.

"Are we taking him to the hotel?"

"No," Clint said, "I don't want him in our room. He stinks, and I don't trust him."

"Well, I do!"

Clint stopped in the middle of the street. "You want to share your room with him?"

"Of course!" Milly cried. "He's my brother!"

"Fine," Clint said, marching over to the nearest horse trough, where he dumped the man.

Jackson Lane took to water with about as much joy as your everyday alley cat. He went under, and he came up scratching and clawing, yelling and hollering.

Clint put his hands on his hips and shook his head. "Milly, I promised I'd help you find him, and I have. Now, I'm gone."

"But . . . but you can't just leave us like this! You heard what the deputy said."

"I sure did. You got your own horse and that chestnut packhorse. Load up that worthless brother of yours and head south. Get him back to Texas if you can."

Milly rushed over to Clint's side. Her eyes were glistening. "Then . . . then this is the end for us?"

"Looks like."

"But . . . but I thought we had love between us."

Clint's anger and resolve bled away quickly. "Listen," he said, lowering his voice and watching Jackson Lane pull himself out of the horse trough and look around as if he were trying to sight in a target to attack, "we did have some love. But not enough. Go home and marry Ben Bandy."

"Yeah," Milly said. "I guess that's what I ought to do."

"It sure as the hell is," Clint said, feeling rotten inside. "Good-bye, Milly."

Tears were welling up in her eyes, and before he completely weakened, Clint turned on his boot heel and headed down the street.

He was putting Milly out of his life. It felt damned bad, but in his heart the Gunsmith was sure it was best thing to do all the way around.

TWELVE

Milly sat on her bed and studied the angry face of her brother, Jackson. She had always considered him to be extremely handsome, but in the harsh light of morning she could see now that he had squandered his good looks with too much whiskey and hard living. He was not yet thirty but looked forty. His eyes were bloodshot, and his hair was long and greasy. His nose had been broken so many times it was squashed, and there was a livid, ugly scar across his right cheek.

"What's happened to you?" Milly whispered. "What have you done to yourself?"

He glared at her from across the room. Even from a distance, he smelled of vomit, bad whiskey, and bad women. "What the hell is *that* supposed to mean?"

"I mean, I remember when you looked and acted like . . . like a kid," she blurted, feeling stupid. "You were always funny."

"Funny?" he echoed. "Oh, yeah, laughing on the inside, bleeding to death on the outside. That's the way they knew me in dear old Huggins, Texas, where Pa could do no wrong."

"But that all changed! You saw Pa go down to whiskey. You didn't try to stop him or—"

"Stop him! Ha!" Jackson shouted, his voice almost breaking with hatred. "I prayed every night that he'd die."

"Stop it!" Milly cried.

"Well, I did! You were his little pet. I was his goddamn whipping boy, and I hated him."

"He loved you!"

Again Jackson laughed, and it was a terrible sound. "Loved me? Well, he sure as hell had a funny way of showing it! He beat the hell out of me after Ma died. Beat me and humiliated me. My only regret is that I wasn't there to piss on his dying body."

"Stop it!" Milly cried again, coming to her feet. "Pa was a better man than you'll ever be!"

"Then that explains why I'm such a stinking failure, doesn't it," Jackson said, his dissipated face alive with loathing.

He glanced wildly around the room, and in doing so, he almost lost his balance and fell. Milly realized that her brother was still drunk.

"You got any whiskey?" He advanced on her a step, fists knotted. "Where do you keep it?"

She shook her head. "I wouldn't have it in my room. It's been the ruin of Pa, and now of you."

Jackson staggered forward. Milly shrank back. "Don't you touch me!"

He lashed out at her, and his knuckles connected solidly. Milly felt herself strike the wall and go down. For a moment she lost her senses, and then she shook her head and looked up at him.

"I should have never come here!" she said, choking with a mixture of anger and fear. "I should have listened to everyone and let you go to hell!"

"Oh, yeah!" He bent down and grabbed her by the hair, and Milly came up clawing at his face. She raked it deeply with her fingernails, and he howled with pain and slung her across the room again.

Milly wanted a gun. She had one, but it was in her bag, and that was too far to reach.

He wiped his hands across his cheek. "You bitch," he breathed. "You always were so damned high and mighty. You played the little princess role, and Pa, he thought you could do no wrong. But I knew better. I knew all you wanted was the ranch."

"That's a lie! I came to tell you it was as much yours as mine!"

"Oh, yeah? Well, what's left of it? Will you answer me *that*?" he challenged, advancing on her.

Milly shrank back toward the window. "Stay away from me, Jackson!"

He stopped. "How many cattle do we have left? And horses? How many of them?"

"None," she blurted. "Pa gambled away everything. He would have lost the land, too, except that Clint—"

"Is he the sonofabitch that threw me in the horse trough so the whole damn town could laugh and make fun of me?"

Milly swallowed. She felt her blood run cold. There was a craziness in Jackson's eyes that she recognized because it was the same craziness she'd seen in her father's eyes when he was drunk and vicious.

"Please, go away."

"I asked you a damn question! Was he the one that dropped me in the horse trough?"

"Yes, but—"

Jackson jumped forward and grabbed her. He grinned and laughed at her terror. "And he's the one that's been screwin' you, my little lily-white, can-do-no-wrong virgin sister. Right?"

"Please."

"Answer me! He was humping you, right?"

"I love him!"

Jackson's lips drew back. He threw his head back and howled like a crazy man. "So you ain't nothing but a whore, just like all the others! My little sister, a stinking, holier-than-thou little—"

Milly snapped. She knew that he was crazy with rage and

that he would even kill her if she didn't escape. She tried to break loose, but he was incredibly strong.

"I'm going to cut off his balls and make you eat them like grapes!" Jackson cackled.

Milly slammed her knee up between his legs, and she saw his mouth fly open and felt his hands lose their grip.

In that instant she thought she could escape, and she tore herself free. But somehow he had the strength and luck to deliver a sledgehammer blow to the side of her head.

Milly felt herself slam backward, and then she heard the sound of breaking glass as she crashed through the second-floor hotel window.

As she fell, she also heard her own scream fill her throat, and that's the last thing she remembered before she struck the boardwalk.

Jackson staggered to the window. He saw people freeze on the street and then rush to surround his sister. He willed her to move, to look up at him, and when she did not, a cry of anguish filled his own throat.

He passed his hand shakily before his eyes and saw a man look up and point his finger.

"That's her brother. *He* must have done it!"

Now everyone looked up, and Jackson recoiled, staggered backward, then grabbed his sister's purse. Tearing it open, he found a roll of greenbacks. Then he turned and bolted out the door.

He bounced off walls as he raced toward the stairs, but when he heard angry shouts from the lobby, he reversed direction and ran to the back of the hall, where he kicked in a door.

The room was empty. Jackson charged across it, threw open the window, and looked down into the alley. He hesitated for only an instant before he climbed through, hung by his fingertips, and then dropped.

Fortunately, he landed and rolled. Coming to his feet, he staggered down the alley, still hearing shouts. Goddamn

Milly and her friend! They had ruined everything! He was finished in this town.

Jackson plunged headlong down the alley. He had friends. Whores who would hide him until he could escape on a fast horse.

He'd go north and hunt mustangs. That's what he'd wanted to do anyway, and now he had money for supplies.

Sure!

At the end of the alley, Jackson staggered to a halt. He realized that he was crying. Why? For his sanctimonious sister. Don't be a fool!

"I hope she's as dead as Pa," he hissed, seeing that the coast was clear and bolting across the street and down into the sleaziest part of Denver, where he knew people would do anything for a price.

It was going to be all right, he told himself. It was going to be just fine. He'd stop drinking so much. He'd catch wild mustangs, start his own damn ranch, and, unlike his pa, he'd hang on to it!

As he paused behind a dilapidated whorehouse, Jackson closed his eyes and felt tears stream down his dirty cheeks.

"Gawdamn this shitty world!" he choked. "I hate it!"

And then he staggered on, where he could find safety and a bottle.

THIRTEEN

The Gunsmith left Denver and rode directly west up the sloping flanks of the Rocky Mountains. Soon the air was cool and he was among the pines. At midday, Clint dismounted beside a sparkling mountain stream and let Duke drink his fill.

"That Rocky Mountain water is the best I ever drank," Clint said after swallowing it.

He removed his shirt and hat, then ducked his head and shoulders into the stream and scrubbed himself vigorously. Clint hobbled Duke and let the animal graze of the high meadow grass. He laid down and gazed up through the whispering pines, watching an eagle soar over the foothill valleys.

"I miss her," he told the black gelding. "I really do. A woman like Milly can get under a man's skin in a hurry if he isn't on guard of himself. I miss her, but it's nice to finally be rid of that whole mess."

Having made this heartfelt declaration, the Gunsmith closed his eyes and dozed for another hour before a blue jay's raucous call awakened him.

Clint tightened his cinch, removed Duke's hobbles, and

rebridled the horse before he mounted and continued on into the mountains.

For some reason he decided not to head for Central City but took the other fork and rode on until he came to a little settlement called Last Chance. It wasn't much of a town. Just two saloons and a couple of other businesses.

"Howdy, mister," a woman called from the front porch of the Ophir Saloon. "You looking for a little action?"

Clint reined Duke in. "I'm always looking for action," he said, sizing up the woman as being a shade hard but still pretty. "What kind of action do you have in mind?"

The woman cocked her hip out and showed Clint a shapely ankle. The dress she was wearing sported a revealing neckline, and Clint was almost interested in seeing more. Almost, but not quite.

"I can give you any kind of action you've a mind—and a money—to pay for," the girl said in her most seductive voice.

"I think I'll pass," Clint said, suddenly unwilling to get involved with another woman so soon after Milly. "Maybe next time, though."

The girl's smile died. "Might not be a 'next time,' mister. A man like you looks like the kind that would be able to see that plain enough."

Clint tipped his hat. "Good day, miss."

He rode on, hearing the girl cuss him good. He didn't give a damn, and later that afternoon, when he saw her again, she had two drunken cowboys, one on each arm.

"See," she called, "I sure didn't need you one damned bit!"

"You're right," Clint said, sipping a beer and taking a chair on the boardwalk where he could watch what was shaping up to be a very pretty sunset.

The Gunsmith spent the next hour in quiet reflection, and just when he was thinking he might mosey back into the Ophir Saloon and see if he could find a decent card game, he saw a man come flogging his horse up the street. He was a poor rider, and was bouncing all over his saddle. For a man like that to run a horse as he was doing, Clint figured he must have had some kind of burr under his saddle.

"Clint Adams!" the man shouted, twisting his head from side to side as the townspeople gawked. "I'm looking for Clint Adams!"

The Gunsmith carefully placed his beer down beside his chair and squinted into the setting sun. "It's that hotelman Bill Baker," he said to himself. "Now what? . . . Over here!"

The man spotted him and reined his heavily lathered horse over to the nearest hitching rail. In a clumsy dismount, he went sprawling into the dirt. Clint hurried over to pick the man up.

"What the hell is wrong with you, Bill?"

The man gripped Clint's arms. "A terrible, terrible thing happened to Milly."

Clint stiffened. "What!"

"It was that sonofabitchin' brother of hers!" Baker swore. "He beat her up in her room, then knocked her clean out the window. She got cut up, and when she hit the ground, the doc thinks she broke something inside."

Baker looked up into Clint's eyes, and the man was crying. "She's callin' your name, Clint! She keeps callin' *your* name! She needs to see you!"

"All right," Clint said, his voice hard and flat, "just take it easy. You and that horse look about half dead."

"But—"

"Here," Clint said, shoving his hotel key into the man's fist. "You have your horse cooled down and taken care of real good. Spend the night in my room and don't start back until tomorrow."

"But—"

Clint silenced the man's protest. "It won't do a bit of good or help Milly if you kill yourself or that horse, now, will it?"

The man shook his head. He sniffled. "It was awful," he said, swallowing painfully. "The glass cut her up pretty good. I didn't see her fall, but someone who did said she didn't make a sound all the way down. She's in Doc Barling's office."

"I know where it is. But don't talk or think about Miss Lane any more than you have to," Clint urged. "Just know that she's going to be all right."

"Will you leave right away?"

"As soon as I go back up to my room and get my things," Clint said. "Come along. When I go for my horse, I'll see that your horse is taken care of."

"Thanks," Baker said.

On the way up to his room, Clint learned all the details, though there were few. Apparently there was no question that it had been Milly's crazy brother who'd thrown or knocked her out of the window. Plenty of witnesses had seen the man's ravaged face.

"Any idea where he is now?"

"No. The sheriff and his deputy have been searching everywhere. Even went through the red-light district. Nothing. If Jackson is still in Denver, he's being hid. Good thing, too. The people are so mad they'd lynch him on sight."

Clint barged into his hotel room, grabbed his saddlebags, and then headed back out the door. "You stay here," he ordered. "Rest up."

"But where's my horse going to be?"

"There's what passes as a stable up at the north end of town. You'll find it. And don't worry!"

Clint left the man and was back in his own saddle within twenty minutes. His expression was grim as the sun plunged behind the high mountain peaks. He figured it would take most of the night to return to Denver, and he prayed that Milly would still be alive to see tomorrow's dawn.

An exhausted horse and rider trotted into Denver about four o'clock the next morning, and Clint rode directly to Doc Barling's office one block south of Larimer Street.

The lights were on, and when Clint knocked on the physician's door, Doc Barling was slow to answer. He was a middle-aged man, calm and competent, with a wild shock of prematurely gray hair. He wore wire-rimmed glasses, and Clint knew that he was well respected by the citizens of Denver.

At the sight of the Gunsmith, the doctor's weary face brightened a little. "Thank heavens he found you."

"Is she still . . ." Clint had trouble finishing the sentence.

"Yes, she's alive and out of danger," the doc said. "But I'm afraid she was cut up pretty badly, and she broke her hip when she landed in the street."

"Will she heal all right?"

"She might have a limp the rest of her life," the doctor said grimly. "I can't say for sure. As for the glass cuts, the Lord must have been watching over her, because she took most of them on the arms, shoulders and thighs. She very nearly bled to death before I could get them all stopped."

Clint exhaled a deep breath. "Maybe I'd better come back a little later, when she's awake."

"She's awake right now, which is surprising, since she is heavily sedated for pain with laudanum," the doctor said. "She is visiting with my missus."

"You sure it's all right?"

"Of course." The doctor motioned for Clint to follow him into the next room.

At the sight of the Gunsmith, Milly sqealed with joy and raised her heavily bandaged hands and arms. Clint sat down beside her on the bed, and Mrs. Barling said, "I think I'll leave you two alone to visit."

"You get some rest yourself," Milly said weakly.

"I will."

When they were alone, Milly looked up at Clint. "I was afraid that Bill would never find you."

"He did. I came as fast as I could," Clint said, trying not to think about what he would do to her brother when the man was found. "What exactly happened?"

Milly told him, leaving out nothing. When she was finished, she added, "He's gone crazy. Just like Pa. He would have killed me sooner or later, Clint. I want you to find him and make sure that he is sent to prison before someone else is hurt."

"I understand that the sheriff has been looking everywhere for him."

"Yes. And a mob." Milly tried to squeeze Clint's hand but was hampered by the bandages. "Clint, a mob will hang him or shoot on sight."

"Sounds like he deserves either one," Clint said.

"No!" Milly lowered her voice. "You were a lawman. You respect the law too much to say that. I need your help. You're the only one that might be able to find him before he is killed."

"And that's why you sent for me?"

"Uh-huh."

"Okay," he heard himself tell her. "I'll go hunting for your brother and I'll try and take him alive. But if he won't surrender, then I'll have to kill him myself."

Milly struggled to retain her composure. "I know that. But you're a dead shot. You would put a bullet through his brain so that he wouldn't suffer. But vigilantes"—Milly shuddered—"they'd terrorize or hurt him very badly before they . . ."

The girl began to sob, and Clint leaned forward and kissed her cheek. "Milly," he said, "I'll try to save your brother's life, but I make no promises."

"Just find him before they do," she whispered. "And then, when this is all over, help me get back to my ranch in Huggins. Ben will take care of me, won't he?"

"Sure he will!" Clint forced a smile. "Ben loves you, and you'll still be the prettiest girl in West Texas."

"Doc says I might never be able to run or even ride a horse. He says my hip is shattered."

"It will heal. You'll not only be able to run and ride, but you'll dance with Ben on your wedding day!"

She managed a brave smile. "You are so good, Clint. And if only you were the marrying kind, why, I'd—"

Clint placed his finger over her lips. "I've got to go and find Jackson," he told her. "I'll be back when it's over."

Milly kissed his finger and nodded. "Don't take any chances. Please?"

"Don't worry," the Gunsmith promised. "Everything is going to be all right."

FOURTEEN

When he left Milly, Clint went straight to the sheriff's office, where he banged on the door until a light went on.

"Who the hell is it at this hour?" challenged the familiar voice of Deputy Holland.

"It's me, Clint Adams. Open up!"

"Adams! You better get the hell out of here and let me go back to sleep or—"

The Gunsmith didn't wait to hear what the man would do because he reared back and kicked the door twice until it threatened to be torn from its hinges.

"All right! All right! You're under arrest!" the deputy shouted, unbolting the door and throwing it open.

Clint grabbed the man and hurled him back across the room. He slammed the door shut behind him. "All right," he snapped, "tell me what you've managed to find out about Jackson Lane's whereabouts."

Deputy Holland was dressed in nothing but a pair of shorts, and when he noted the steel in the Gunsmith's eyes, he lost his backbone.

"He must have managed to get out of Denver. We've

looked everyplace. No one has seen or heard of him since he got away."

"Well, that's just great," Clint said angrily. "Does anyone even have an idea where he might have gone?"

The deputy shook his head. "Did the girl tell you her brother took her money?"

"No."

"Well, he did. Jackson was a bad one, and I thought sure he'd go on a drinking and gambling spree, but he didn't. I guess he might even think that he killed his sister and that he had to run."

"Damnation!" Clint swore. "I mean to find the man and bring him to justice."

"Why not let him go?" Holland said. "He won't ever come back. Jackson is crazy, but he's smart, if you know what I mean."

"Yeah, I know what you mean," Clint said. "And maybe he wouldn't return to your town, but sooner or later, when he was down and out, he'd return to Huggins, Texas."

"So?"

"So he'd make life hell for his sister. Maybe get drunk and go crazy again and really kill her the next time."

Clint turned toward the door, but hesitated. "I want to know who was his favorite woman."

"I already talked to her."

"*I* want to talk to her."

The deputy retreated a step and managed to bluster, "I thought sure we'd seen the last of you. I wish we had. You got no authority in Denver. None at all!"

Clint's hand flashed to the gun at his side. It came up, and he shoved the barrel down the man's shorts, cocked the hammer back, and said, "Freeze!"

Deputy Holland's eyes bugged with terror. His jaw dropped, and he raised up on his bare toes. "Please!" he cried. "No!"

Clint smiled menacingly. "You're quitting your job and leaving town come first daybreak. Isn't that right?"

"Yes!"

Clint removed his Colt from the man's shorts and lowered the hammer. Deputy Holland's knees were quaking so badly that they would not support him, and he had to stagger over to the sheriff's desk chair, where he collapsed.

"Goddamn you!" Holland breathed shakily. "Her name is Babette."

"Last name?"

"She's a dance-hall girl! They don't have last names."

"Where can I find her?"

"Yellow Bird Saloon. It's over in the toughest part of town, where I hope someone will bury a knife in your liver."

"Be out of here at first light," Clint warned, "and I better never hear of you wearing another lawman's badge. Not in Denver and not in any other town."

Clint left the sheriff's office and headed for his horse. He knew that no one would be awake in the red-light district at this hour, but that was their problem, not his.

"We'll get this over with before noon and I'll have you back in a stall shortly after," he promised.

Duke nickered softly. The black gelding's coat was crusted with drying sweat, and Clint knew the animal was tired and hungry.

Well, so was he, but if Jackson Lane was still skulking around Denver, he was in for a world of trouble.

As Clint had expected, the Yellow Bird Saloon was locked up tight and would probably remain so at least until noon. Clint rode completely around the building and saw that there were several little shacks attached to its back wall. He was sure that Jackson Lane would not be stupid enough to be inside one of them, but perhaps his favorite girl would have a clue as to the man's whereabouts.

Clint dismounted and walked stiffly up to the nearest shack, where he banged on the door.

"Go away!" came a sleepy woman's voice from inside.

Clint tried the door handle, but it was solidly locked and

he could not budge it even a little. "I've got to talk to Babette. Is that you, Miss?"

"Go away!"

"If it's you, we need to talk about Jackson."

"Damn you, I've got nothing to say about him. He's gone! I ain't seen him in over a week. Now let me go back to sleep."

"Not until we talk first."

"I've already talked to Deputy Holland. Now, go away!"

"I'm going to pull my gun and shoot off the door if you don't open it."

Clint heard Babette knock over something that shattered. He stepped to one side of the door in case the dance-hall girl came out with a gun in her own fist.

"All right!" she swore, shoving the door open to reveal herself in a silk wrapper that clung so tightly to her body that it left nothing whatsoever to the imagination. "What the hell do you want to ask me that can't wait until this afternoon?"

"I want to know if you have any idea where he might be hiding."

"No, I don't."

Babette attempted to grab the door and slam it shut, but Clint caught her arm. "Mind if I have a look inside?"

"Yes."

"I'm afraid that I need to look anyway," Clint said, pushing past the girl with his gun clenched solidly in his fist.

The little shack was surprisingly clean, and Babette really was sleeping alone.

"Satisfied?" she asked when he stepped back outside.

"No, and I won't be until I catch Jackson Lane."

"Why, so you can gun him down before the vigilantes hang him?" she asked sarcastically.

"I mean to take him before a judge and see that he goes to prison for what he did to his sister."

"Oh, little Miss Purity? Well, from what I hear, she deserved to be thrown out the window."

It was all that Clint could do not to lose his temper. Clenching his hands at his sides, he said, "If Jackson comes back, you tell him I'm his only chance—not that he deserves one."

When the girl stepped back inside and tried a second time to close the door, Clint held it up a moment. "You tell him my name is Clint Adams. I'll see that he gets prison time instead of a noose or a bullet."

"Yeah," she said, curling her lip with contempt. "If I ever see Jackson, I'll be sure and pass your generous offer along."

Clint released the door, and Babette slammed it shut in his face. The Gunsmith shook his head sadly. He was sure that Babette was lying. If so, that meant he'd have to keep a close eye on her until Jackson came to her for help.

And he would. Scum like Jackson Lane always crawled under the door looking for sympathy and a handout. The saddest part, though, was that they nearly always found a foolish young woman like Babette to pull down to their own slimy level of existence.

"I'll be around," he said under his breath as he strode wearily back toward his horse.

FIFTEEN

That same afternoon, Clint sent a telegram to a good friend in El Paso, asking him please to forward a message to Ben Bandy in Huggins. Clint's request was that word reach Bandy that Milly had been seriously injured and needed him by her side.

When Clint left the telegraph office, he had some breakfast, then moseyed on back to the sheriff's office. He was not surprised to find that Sheriff Stanley Yates was in a grouchy mood.

"My goddamn deputy just up and quit on me last night. Left a message saying I was supposed to forward his wages to Santa Fe!"

"Humph," Clint mused. "Well, I kept telling you that he was a bad one. You're better off without him, Sheriff."

Yates did not look convinced. "This is too damn big a town for one man to police. I need a deputy."

"Then find one," Clint said with little sympathy in his heart. "Only the next time, pick a man who has learned to use his brain before his mouth."

"Otis had his faults," the sheriff conceded, "and he could get into trouble. But he was a hard worker, and he had guts.

He never backed down from anybody."

Clint decided it would not be smart to argue this point. Shifting the subject, he asked, "Any leads on where Jackson Lane might have gone?"

"I think he's flown the coop," Yates said. "My guess is that he went north to do that mustanging he kept talking about."

"I paid a visit to his girlfriend."

"Babette?"

"Yeah."

"Bet she didn't tell you any more than she told me," the sheriff said, plopping down in his office chair. "That girl sure isn't very friendly, but she's kind of pretty."

"I think she knows where Jackson is hiding," Clint said. "And I think he's still in Denver."

"Aw, bullshit!" The sheriff threw his legs up on his desk. "Now, don't give me that kind of talk. We searched damn near every stinking hole in that part of town, and nobody has seen him since he knocked his sister through the second-story window."

"We'll see about that," Clint said, unconvinced. "I'm going to keep a close watch on Babette over the next few days. If she's helping to hide him, then she'll lead me to wherever it is he's hiding."

"You do what you want. Just remember that I want the man to stand trial. That means you don't gun him down, right?"

"Of course," Clint said, forcing a grin.

"You ought to go back to wherever you came from," the sheriff called as the Gunsmith moved toward the front door.

"Thanks," Clint said as he went outside and headed toward the doctor's office to see Milly. "Thanks for your kind words and cooperation."

"Go to hell!" Yates shouted.

Clint's lips formed a tight smile as he made his way back to see how Milly was getting along. When he came to the doctor's office, Clint went right inside and found Milly sitting up in bed while the doctor's wife was feeding her a piece of toast along with some coffee.

"Why don't you let me take over," Clint said.

"Thank you."

When they were alone, Clint leaned over and kissed Milly on the cheek. "You like being spoon-fed like this?"

"No."

"Won't be much longer. I'm sure that those bandages will be coming off your hands soon. And by then I expect that Ben will be here to take over."

"Ben?"

Clint nodded. "I sent for him, Milly. I want him to take you home. You don't belong in Denver any more than I do."

"But what about Jackson?"

"He's my problem," Clint told her. "I'm going to find and bring him to justice."

For the next few minutes Clint told Milly everything he'd learned about her brother's possible whereabouts. "And so," he ended, "I just have a feeling that your brother is still hiding in this town and that Babette will soon be leading me to him."

Milly nodded but did not seem excited about this piece of news. "I wish you would just let him go away."

"Not a chance," Clint told her. "Your brother isn't the boy you once knew. He's turned into a dangerous man. Maybe a long prison sentence will even straighten him out. One thing for sure: It would get him sober and allow him to think clearly, perhaps for the first time in many years."

"Yeah," Milly had to agree.

"Hey," Clint said, raising her chin, "you did everything you could to be fair to your brother. And what did he do in repayment other than try to kill you?"

"I don't think he really tried to kill me at all," Milly said. "I think he just lost his temper and was as surprised as I was when I went through that glass window."

Clint shook his head. "Love can be so blind. And if that was the case, why didn't he come down to be at your side instead of running away?"

"He was scared," Milly said. "He was afraid that someone might kill him."

Clint knew there was no point in arguing with this girl. "I better be going."

"Aren't you even going to finish feeding me my toast and coffee?"

"Of course."

When Milly was finished, Clint rose to leave, but Milly called, "How long before you think that Ben might be here?"

"Two, maybe three weeks at the most. I'm sure he'll drop everything and come the minute he gets the message."

"Yes, he will," Milly said. "Did you tell him anything about my scars and my hip?"

Clint shook his head. "It won't make any difference."

"I hope you're right."

"I know I am," Clint said.

"I'll have these damned bandages off my hands and arms by then. And these other cuts, they'll be well on the mend. I just hope the scars don't turn out too ugly."

"It won't matter to him," Clint said. "There's not a scratch on your face, and you're still the prettiest girl in Texas."

Milly brightened, and her blue eyes danced. "And you're still the handsomest lover I ever had."

Clint felt his cheeks warm, and when he turned and walked out of Milly's room, he swore he could hear her soft laughter.

For the next week, Clint stayed as close as he could to Babette without being seen. He rented a little room only a few hundred feet from Babette's shack, and when she went to work in the Yellow Bird Saloon at night, he slipped in among the rough crowd, kept his Stetson pulled down low, and followed her every move.

Two things surprised him about the young dance-hall girl: One, she had real talent and a voice that, had it been trained, would have been of opera quality, and two, she was clean. By that Clint meant that she did not get drunk, like so many of the girls who sang and danced in places like this, and she did not sell her body every night to the highest bidder. In fact, when Babette finished up her last song and dance at about two in the morning, she was escorted by a couple of the saloon's strongmen so that no harm came to her from some overzealous fan.

The more that Clint watched the girl, the more of a mystery she became. And not once, in the entire first week he kept her under surveillance, did she give any indication that Jackson Lane was hiding in Denver.

"I don't know what to think," Clint confessed one afternoon as he sat beside Milly's bed. "I usually judge a person pretty well, but this one might have fooled me when she said she didn't know where your brother was hiding."

"Why don't you give it just a few more days?"

"I might as well," Clint said. "Because I sure haven't any other leads to follow. If he's not in Denver, then I haven't a clue where to begin looking."

"If he isn't in Denver, let him go," Milly said quietly. "I know that you think he'd show up someday down in Huggins and ruin my life, but I think you're wrong."

Clint had no interest in arguing with Milly. She had a soft place in her heart for her dissolute brother, and nothing was going to change her mind, not even the fact that he'd knocked her through a second-story window and left her to bleed to death in the street below.

"A couple more days," Clint said. "If I don't get some indication by then that your brother is still in Denver, I'm pulling stakes."

"All right," Milly said. "And maybe by then Ben will be here."

"I hope so," Clint said, less than satisfied with the way things were going for them.

But that evening shortly after midnight, Clint saw a shadowy figure lurking in the wings of the stage on which

Babette performed. She was singing "My Love Is a Red, Red Rose" when Clint first saw the figure appear. After her song, Babette waved and bowed. Then, before the Gunsmith could rush around to position himself behind the stage, the pretty dance-hall girl was gone.

SIXTEEN

For several minutes Clint was frantic, wondering where Babette had gone and if the shadowy figure he'd seen lurking behind the stage curtains was, indeed, Jackson Lane.

"Where'd she go?" he demanded of the man who worked the curtains during Babette's performances.

"Who?"

"Babette, of course!"

"Why, to her dressing room, of course. But you aren't allowed to . . ."

Clint didn't wait to hear the rest. He spied the "dressing room" which was no more than a large, open-topped wooden box with a door.

"Hey, come back here!" the man shouted.

But Clint was already rushing down to the dressing room and grabbing the handle of the door. It was locked from the inside.

"Open up!"

"Who is it?"

Clint knew better than to reveal his identity. If Jackson Lane were hiding inside, there was no telling what the man might do when cornered.

"There's a fire out here! You need to go outside until we get it under control!"

Clint thought for sure that he heard a male voice inside.

"Who are you?" Babette cried.

"Open up!"

Clint grabbed the door handle and tried to rip it open. He was sure that Jackson was inside!

The door sprang open so unexpectedly that Clint was thrown backward. He lit on his backside and went skidding across the floor, watching as Jackson and Babette bolted from the dressing room and disappeared through a back door.

"Damn!" Clint shouted, jumping up and charging after the pair.

He slammed out of the alley just in time to see the two disappear around a dim corner. Clint charged after them, and when he rounded the same corner, he saw he was rapidly closing the distance as they raced down yet another alley in Denver's worst shantytown.

Yanking his six-gun out of his holster, Clint raised it and fired into the sky. "Halt! Halt or I'll shoot!"

Jackson halted, all right, but as he did, he pulled his own six-gun and grabbed Babette to pull her close to his chest as a shield.

"*You* drop it, mister! Now!"

Clint skidded to a halt, hearing Babette cry, "Damn you, Jackson, is this the thanks I get for saving you from a lynch mob?"

"Shut up!"

When Babette fought and tried to bite his arm, Jackson pistol-whipped her. Clint saw the woman's legs buckle, but Jackson was too smart to let her fall.

"I said drop your gun!" Jackson hissed. "Drop it or I'll kill her, then you."

Clint knew he was beaten. He had no choice whatsoever but to drop his six-gun.

Jackson dropped Babette unceremoniously in the dirt. Clint saw she was still conscious, she even raised her head and stared at him, but the woman was dazed and Clint knew that there was nothing he could do to stop whatever would happen next.

"Who the hell are you?" Jackson demanded, walking a little unsteadily and smelling of liquor.

"Does it make any difference?" Clint asked. "Haven't you already made up your mind to kill me?"

Jackson's face, haggard in the moonlight, split into a cruel grin. "I guess I have at that. But I still want to know."

"I brought your sister to Denver," Clint said. "She had some half-baked idea that you were worth salvaging. Everyone who knew you from Huggins told her you'd never change, that you were worthless, but she didn't believe them."

At the mention of his sister, Jackson's expression turned bitter. "I never wanted to see her or Pa again! Why didn't she just leave me the hell alone?"

"She thought it only fair to tell you that your father died leaving you half the ranch."

Jackson barked a mean laugh. "Hell, there was nothing left of it. Nothing but the land, mostly worthless ground."

"So you knocked her out the window. Is that the way you repaid her for trying to be honest?"

"I didn't mean to! She had no damn business coming here!"

Clint said nothing because there was nothing left to say.

"You slept with my sister, didn't you," Jackson said with a sly grin.

"What the hell kind of question is that?"

"Answer me! Was the great virgin a good lay?"

Clint's hands clenched at his sides. "You sick sonofabitch, do what you're going to do."

Jackson raised the gun and cocked the hammer. "You *did* sleep with her! I can tell by the way you're acting."

"Go to hell!"

Clint saw Jackson's face contort with hatred as the gun in the man's fist raised to a level with his eyes. Jackson's hand shook as he began to squeeze the trigger. And rather than take a bullet square in the face, Clint dove for Jackson's knees, knowing he didn't have a prayer of saving his own life.

Clint felt a million needles drive through his eye sockets, accompanied by a brilliant light that seared his brain. Dimly he heard a scream and wondered if it was his own.

"Hang on!" Babette cried, throwing herself down beside him.

Clint tried. He felt the woman cradle his head and heard her begin to call for a doctor, for someone to help—anyone!

The light that filled his skull dimmed, and the pain and roaring in his ears fell silent. As the Gunsmith looked up at the woman's face, he saw that the stars were spinning in the heavens.

"Why did you throw down your gun to save my life?" she kept asking him. "Why?"

Clint tried to tell her that it was a matter of honor. Foolish honor, perhaps, but it was his code, and he knew he could not have played this out any differently and been able to live with himself. Only now, he was not at all sure he would be alive much longer.

"Who the hell are you?" she was asking him. "I must know your name!"

His lips formed an answer, but his tongue seemed paralyzed, and he could not speak. So she lay his head back down on the dirt.

"I've got to go for a doctor," she said, swaying on her feet.

He realized then that her own head was bleeding. Clint wanted to tell Babette that he preferred to die cradled in her lap and that she should stay until he was gone.

"I won't be away but a few minutes," she said, "you just have to hold on."

Somehow he managed to nod, showing her he understood.

Then she was staggering up the alley, and he closed his eyes when she disappeared, leaving him alone lying in filth, smelling rotten garbage.

• • •

Clint awoke the following morning with the worst head-ache he'd ever had in his life. Babette was at his side, and so was Milly, with most of her bandages removed.

"Where am I?" he asked groggily, seeing them in double images.

"You're in the Denver Hotel," Babette said. "Best room in the whole damn city."

"Babette insisted on it," Milly said. "She also paid for my room right across the hall, though I told her not to."

"I wanted to," Babette said. "I figure I've messed things up about as bad as possible hiding your brother, Miss Lane. If I'd let the vigilantes have him right after he knocked you through the window, none of this would have happened."

"It wasn't your fault. You loved him, too," Milly said in a small voice.

Clint squinted up at both of them. They were as handsome a pair of women as could be found, but they sure had been fools when it came to judging the character of Jackson Lane.

"Did he get away again?" Clint managed to asked through clenched teeth.

"Yes," Babette said. "And this time he really did leave town on the run."

"I'm going to get him if . . . ahh!" Clint cried, falling back to his pillow and cradling his splitting skull. "What happened?"

"Doctor says you have a wicked concussion. Says the bullet from Jackson's gun put a furrow in your skull that would match up with those in a Nebraska cornfield. He said that if the bullet had gone just a fraction of an inch deeper, you'd be dead."

"Right now," Clint groaned, wishing he were seeing two women instead of a pair of twins, "I almost wish I was dead. How long will this go on?"

"Doctor Barling said you'd probably be well enough to get up in about a week, but it might take a month before you stopped seeing double."

"A month!" Clint would have sworn out loud, but his exclamation drove another stake through his brain. Instead he whispered, "Jackson will be long gone by then."

"Let him go," Babette pleaded. "He's so crazy that it's only a matter of time before he's shot or hanged."

"Sure it is. But how many people will die by his hand before that happens?"

Neither Babette nor Milly had an answer.

"As soon as I can walk, see straight enough to shoot, and can ride, I'm going after him," Clint vowed. "And I don't care if I have to ride all the way to California!"

SEVENTEEN

In the days that followed, the Gunsmith railed at being confined to bed. Yet, every time he tried even to sit up, he was assailed by waves of head-splitting pain. Milly had recovered well enough to take up residence at the hotel, and if not for Babette's frequent visits, Clint would have been entirely miserable.

Babette brought him candy and read him the newspaper in the early afternoon. "Denver is projected to be the biggest town in Colorado," she told him.

Clint was not overly interested. "I don't care about that," he grumped. "What I want is to get out of this bed and go find Jackson Lane. Every day I waste here is going to make picking up his trail that much more difficult."

"That can't be changed," Babette said philosophically. She had dark brown hair and a pixieish face, with thin eyebrows and a nose that was slightly pugged. "So you might as well try to make the best of the situation."

"How?" he asked. "I can't even sit up without feeling like a spike is being driven through my skull."

"I know," she said, "but I heard you tell the doctor that you no longer have double vision."

"That's true at least," he groused. "How'd you ever get mixed up with someone like Jackson?"

Babette cocked her head a little to one side, as was her habit. "Do you really want to know?"

"Yes."

"I saw him attack two men who were beating an old wagon horse that had stumbled and fallen to its knees just up the street. Jackson loves horses, and even though he took a beating that afternoon, I was so touched by his courage and sympathy that I took him home and nursed his wounds."

Clint managed a thin smile. "First him, now me. At heart you must be a Good Samaritan."

"I'd like to think I am. If I were younger I'd become a doctor. It's a field that is just now opening to women in this country, though there have been women doctors in Europe for at least this century."

"Hmm," Clint said, studying her intelligent, caring face. "So instead of healing, you went into the entertainment business, and sometimes you nurse us unfortunates."

Babette frowned. "I know you'll find it difficult to understand, but when Jackson fought two bullies for mistreating a poor old horse, and when you threw down your gun to save my life, you were both my heroes. And to be very honest, there is a terrible shortage of heroes in this world. Selfless courage, such as you and even Jackson displayed, reaffirm my faith in mankind."

Clint was impressed. "I suppose, singing and dancing every night, you don't see and hear the best side of man's nature."

"That's an understatement." Babette leaned forward and kissed his lips. "It's men like you that keep me from becoming cynical. And for that, I thank you from the bottom of my heart."

Clint reached up and gently pulled her down on the bed beside him. "Doc says that I'm going to have to be here another four or five days. Why don't we see if we can make them special."

She laughed, pulled away a little, and looked into his eyes. Sounding very innocent, she asked, "And just how do you suppose we do that?"

Clint reached down and pulled her dress up to her thighs, which he began to stroke. "Guess."

"Here? Why, Clint Adams! What if the doctor suddenly came over and caught us in your recovery bed?"

"He won't," Clint said, sliding his hand up her leg even higher. "He's gone to deliver a baby south of town. There's no way he can be back before noon. That gives us at least two hours."

"But your head! I don't want you to have a relapse."

He chuckled because she wasn't making it easy, and yet he was sure she wanted to make love just as much as he did.

"I'll keep my head on the pillow," he whispered, slipping his right hand to a place that made her spread her legs and sigh. "I think we can figure out an equally accommodating solution."

She swallowed and kissed his throat, then her lips trailed down to his chest. "Yes," she whispered, "I think we can, too."

Clint only had to pull off the pajama bottoms that Babette had given him, and then he watched hungrily as Babette tore off her own clothing. He threw his bed cover aside and looked up at her with a smile of anticipation.

"And to think that I was dreading the next few days."

Babette was on him in a hurry. She spread her legs wide and impaled herself, then rocked back and forth, moaning softly with pleasure. It felt so good to Clint that he forgot himself and tried to sit up and reach for her large, lush breasts, but that damn, splitting headache drove him back to his pillow.

"Oh," Babette cooed with sympathy, "let me make it feel better."

Clint closed his eyes and let her do things that made the pain go away in a hurry. When he felt a fire starting to build in his loins, he reached up and pulled the woman down on top of him, and they made love faster and faster. Babette was strong and hungry. Her powerful hips were almost punishing as they slammed up and down on Clint's manhood.

"Come on, my hero!" she cried. "Do it to me!"

Clint growled deep in his throat and reached down to grab Babette's heaving buttocks. With his lips pulled back from his teeth, and careful to keep his head flat, he roared and exploded inside the woman.

Babette gasped and then her haunches stiffened and she threw back her head and let her body jerk until she collapsed on the Gunsmith.

Clint smiled and held the woman, feeling her heart pound against his chest. "I think I'm going to live now," he said.

She giggled in his ear. "I'm sure you are. You just needed a little stimulation in order to recover."

"You're the best stimulation I could imagine," he said, "and if—"

"Clint!"

He twisted his head to see Ben Bandy and Milly standing in the doorway, gaping at them. Clint yanked the covers over Babette, but not before the shocked couple had seen their sweaty bodies locked together.

"Clint," Milly said again, this time shaking her head. "And here I was telling Ben that you were practically on your deathbed."

The Gunsmith had never quite been in such a compromising position before, and on one of the rare occasions in his life, he was speechless.

Babette, however, was surprisingly quick to recover. She smiled. "Well, you must be Mr. Ben Bandy, the blacksmith from Huggins, Texas."

"Ben," Milly whispered, jabbing her powerful young fiancé in the ribs hard enough to make him grunt, "close your mouth before you catch a fly!"

Ben's jaw snapped shut. Of the four, he was easily the

most shocked. "Uh . . . yeah," he stammered. "Pleased to meet you, miss."

"Me, too," Babette said cheerily, as if they were attending Denver's social event of the year. "Are you going to be staying in Denver very long?"

"I shouldn't," Ben said almost apologetically. "But we won't leave until Milly is ready. In fact . . . can I tell them, honey?"

"Sure," Milly said, unable to take her eyes off Clint, who was beginning to squirm under her steady gaze and Babette's pressing weight.

"Well," Ben said proudly, "Milly and I have decided to get married right here in Denver and make it sort of our honeymoon. She's already got a fancy hotel room, and we were wondering if you'd both be the best man and the maid of honor."

"I'd love to!" Babette said.

"Me, too," Clint said after gulping, "but could we work out the details a little later?"

Milly laughed. "What's the matter, dear?"

"Well, I'm starting to get this splitting headache."

The next thing Clint knew, both women were laughing, and he felt like a total fool. The only one who looked even more uncomfortable than he felt was Ben, who was trying to get Milly to leave.

When the couple finally did make their exit, Babette could not stop laughing.

"I don't see the humor in this at all," Clint growled.

Babette kissed his mouth, and her hand slipped down to his manhood, which she began to rub against her silky crotch.

"Why don't we just get back to where we were before they stepped in?"

"I don't know," Clint said, still a little unnerved. "It wouldn't surprise me if the doc came by, or failing that, someone else stopped in here."

Babette murmured in his ear and raised her hips over his, teasing him with the heat of her body.

"Do you really think we ought to stop?"

"Damn you," Clint said, unable to suppress a smile, "you and Milly were awful. Poor Ben was beet red and mortified."

"He's got plenty to learn," Babette said, easing down on Clint with a moan of pleasure. "And unless I've judged Milly all wrong, she'll turn that big blacksmith of hers into an insatiable lover."

Clint supposed that Babette was right. "I wonder how long they'll wait until they get married."

"Not long," Babette whispered, her body starting to move in unison with that of the Gunsmith. "In fact, I'll bet after the eyeful we gave them, they're already heading for her room."

Clint smiled at that. Babette was probably right. Milly loved to make love, he knew that for a fact. And as big and powerful as he was, Ben Bandy was going to have his hands full with that passionate young woman.

The Gunsmith's thoughts were jarred away from Ben and Milly by the sound of Babette's soft cries of pleasure. They made him forget all about Milly.

EIGHTEEN

Jackson Lane's hands had stopped shaking, and the raging whiskey thirst that had consumed him for three days after he'd escaped Denver was gone. Now, feeling better than he had in months, Jackson raised up in his stirrups and squinted off toward the distant Big Horn Mountains of Wyoming.

Now, this, he thought, is wild horse country if ever there was. Lots of tall green grass, pine-forested mountains, plenty of clear, cold streams. It was the kind of country that made a man glad he was alive—at least most of the year. Winters could be hard, but Jackson had no intention of finding out just how hard. By October, when the aspen began to blaze with colors, he would be riding south with his pockets filled with mustanging money.

But first Jackson needed to locate a wealthy rancher who would be willing to bankroll his venture. It was never a good idea for a man to use his own money, and what money Jackson had taken from his sister, he meant to keep for himself.

Off in the distance, Jackson could see the outlines of a sizable Wyoming ranch house, and he figured this one was just as good a place to start as any. He touched spurs to his sorrel gelding and galloped across the short green grass, scattering antelope mixed among several thousand head of longhorn cattle.

The ranch looked promising as Jackson grew nearer. He had shaved that very morning and put on a clean shirt. Nothing could be done about his shaggy hair, soiled pants, and faded shirt, but then, a man looking for a job busting broncs or catching wild horses wasn't supposed to look as if he owned a bank.

As Jackson rode into the ranch yard, he was aware of the critical glances he was receiving from the cowboys. Jackson ignored their scrutiny, looking neither to the right nor the left but straight ahead toward the house. Anyway, he knew he was a fine figure on horseback and that his gear was first-rate and his sorrel was worthy of any man's admiration. The cowboys, he was certain, would size him up as a top hand, though they'd be able to see from a few details, like his bit and spurs, that he was from Texas rather than the northern country.

"Hello the house!" Jackson called out, pulling his horse up short but not stepping down until he received an invitation.

Several minutes passed before an older man with white hair, a long handlebar mustache, and a cane in his fist appeared. Right behind him came a girl of about nineteen. She wasn't exactly beautiful and was dressed in a man's shirt and pants, but she wasn't bad-looking either, and her eyes were bold and curious.

"Howdy," Jackson said, tipping his hat to the old rancher and his daughter, perhaps even granddaughter. "My name is . . . Jack Smith. I'm a bronc buster with a different style of breaking a rank horse than you've likely ever seen before. Some who have seen and admired my work with horses say they've never seen better."

The old man had a hard face, with a smallish mouth over-shadowed between heavy brows and a big, aquiline nose. "I got a bronc buster already, Mr. Smith. But if you're hungry and want to spend the night, then we'll be happy to feed you and your horse."

Jackson had not expected any more than this. "Much obliged," he said. Then to the girl, "miss."

She smiled. "I judge you from Texas or maybe New Mexico, cowboy. What are you doing up in this northern county?"

"Just enjoying the beauty and hopin' to catch a few good horses before the snow flies this winter."

"Well," she said, "we've got them. Must be forty or more in that big band that has staked out its territory up along the foothills, huh, Pa?"

"I'd say more like sixty. They're led by a big bay stallion. Sonofabitch must weight over a thousand pounds, and he's meaner than a badger. I'd put a bullet through his gizzard if he wasn't so smart as to stay out of rifle range."

"Maybe you'd like me to catch and geld him," Jackson said easily. "Sometimes the best horses come from the ones that were the worst before they were broke."

"Not in my experience they don't," the rancher said, stepping down from his porch and walking up to Jackson's horse. "My name is Pat Pierce. This is my daughter, Carole."

Jackson again tipped his hat. "I appreciate the offer of your bunkhouse and some vittles, Mr. Pierce. And even if you don't have any use for another bronc buster, I'd like to solve your problem with that bay stallion. I take it he's probably been stealing your good mares."

"That's right. He's got more than he can handle right now, but he's like most of the male population that away, I suppose."

Pierce winked and looked at his daughter, who said, "Aw, cut it out, Pa! That stallion is just doing what comes natural for him."

"Well, his 'natural' is costing me good saddle horses," the rancher snorted, the humor going out of him. "And Mr. Smith, if you can rid me of his ornery hide—take him alive or dead, I don't care—then I'll pay you one hundred dollars for your trouble."

"Well, thank you, sir! Come tomorrow right after breakfast, I'll ride up there and start scouting around."

"You do that," the rancher said with a smile before he turned around and stumped painfully back into his ranch house.

Carole came down from the porch. "I think I could save you some time by showing you where that stallion and his mares drink and hide. I'll ride out with you after breakfast."

"No need to trouble yourself, miss. I've had some experience tracking mustangs. I know horses."

"I'm sure," she said. "But I still think it will save you a lot of time."

"Suit yourself, miss."

She gave him a sultry half smile that set his mind to racing, and then she turned around and sashayed back into the ranch house, her bottom nice and round in a pair of tight-fitting pants.

Jackson grinned. He figured he might get more than he bargained for tomorrow when they rode up into the Big Horn Mountains.

"If I was you, Smith," a hard voice said from behind him, "I'd keep my eyes where they belong."

Jackson turned around to face a man his own age with hot eyes and an aggressive cut to his jaw. "You talking to me?"

"I sure as hell am. Keep your eyes off of my girl or I'll close them with my fists."

Jackson's smile froze on his lips. A week ago, hung over and sick from whiskey, he'd have been inclined to ignore this challenge because the cowboy in front of him was tough-looking and at least ten pounds heavier. But now, with a clear head and no shakes, Jackson saw things more clearly.

"The girl didn't ask me if I wanted her along, she told me she was coming. I don't see that it's any of your business anyway, cowboy."

"Maybe I'll make it my business."

Jackson did not want to get into a hard fight right away, so he said, "Why don't you just ride along with us tomorrow if she's your girl?"

The cowboy had not expected this offer and was caught off balance. "Well, I got to help work cattle tomorrow."

"That's a real shame," Jackson said with mock regret. "But don't worry none, I'll take care of Miss Pierce."

"That's what I'm afraid of," the cowboy growled. "Just keep your hands and your eyeballs to yourself or I'll make sure that you ride off stretched across your saddle tomorrow night."

"I'll keep that in mind," Jackson said, reining his horse around and riding toward the nearest corral, where he guessed he was supposed to put his weary horse.

No one said much of anything to him that evening. That was fine with Jackson, who supposed that everyone had heard of the little difference of opinion he was having with the cowboy, whose name turned out to be Ted Matheson and who was the ranch's only full-time bronc buster.

Jackson slept very well that night, and after breakfast the next morning he waved good-bye to old Pat Pierce and rode off to scout mustangs with the rancher's daughter.

Jackson was all business that morning. He said little but instead listened as Carole talked practically nonstop about how hard it was being a young woman on an isolated Wyoming cattle ranch. Jackson listened without any real sympathy. He was reminded of Babette and how hard her life was dancing and singing at a dive like the Yellow Bird Saloon. Now, there had been one hell of a woman.

"So here is where they come down to drink early every morning," Carole was saying as she dismounted and knelt to examine the tracks.

Jackson also dismounted and tied his reins to a piece of brush. He studied the tracks. "How come, if you know this, someone hasn't shot the stallion?"

"They've tried," Carole said, straightening. "But the stallion drives his mares in first and always just before daybreak. Ted and the others have never been able to get a clean shot, and there're some valuable mares in that outlaw's band that Pa won't allow to be shot by accident."

"I see." Jackson tipped his hat back and looked all around. "Do you think the stallion leaves this drinking place along the same trail he uses coming in?"

"I don't think anyone knows," Carole said. "Either the men have tried to ambush him at the water hole and he scatters behind the cover of his mares, or else he bolts and runs through the brush and pines to where no one can get a clean shot."

"I don't want to shoot him," Jackson said. "I mean to capture him alive and break him for you."

She actually laughed. "You've sure got brass, I'll give you that much. You haven't even seen this horse, and already you're promising to do what no one on the payroll could accomplish."

"I'm the best," Jackson said. "I can think like a stallion. I can smell danger, just like them. And I can smell a willing female coming in heat."

Carole blinked, and when Jackson stepped forward and kissed her mouth, she made a big show of struggling in his arms.

Jackson just chuckled. "No sense putting on a show, 'cause nobody is around to watch. Besides, you're ready."

She stopped struggling. "You scare me," she whispered.

"I should," he replied as he pulled her down on the grass and began to kiss her hair, her face, her neck, and then to unbutton her shirt.

"No!" she pleaded.

"You're no virgin, girl. I can tell."

"Damn you, Jack Smith, if my father or Ted finds out about this, they'll have you strung up by your toes and castrated."

Jackson laughed outright, and then he took the ranch girl fast and hard, like the bay would one of his mares in heat.

When he was finished with her, he stood up and buttoned his pants.

"You didn't even give us time to take our boots off," she said petulantly. "You didn't have to do it so rough."

"I think that's why a girl like you wants it."

Carole stood up a little shakily. "We don't have to go back yet. There's still plenty of time before dark."

Jackson almost laughed, but instead he tightened his cinch. "I'd like to get a good look at the stallion and his band today. You know where we might spot them?"

"Yes!" she snapped, going to her own horse as she stuffed her shirt down into her pants and then whacked the dirt and stickers from herself.

"Then let's go get a look-see. If we find them soon enough, I just might have time to service you once more before we head back to your pa's ranch."

"You go straight to hell, Jack Smith!" she hissed. "I'm not ever going to go riding out alone with you again."

He barked a hard laugh. "It's your choice, but I think you'll change your mind in a couple of days. Either way, it's up to you."

She shot him a furious look and climbed onto her horse, then spurred the animal off into the trees.

Jackson swung into the saddle and went after her. He felt better than he had in a long, long time. Whiskey, he knew, was his poison, and when he was in the towns, he couldn't resist its lure. But out here with nothing to drink but clear, cold water and with his lungs full of mountain air, he was really alive once again.

He'd just proven that much to himself—and to that little bitch with the hot pants and big head. Yeah, he'd shown Miss Carole her true stripes, and although she wasn't liking what she'd discovered, she'd be back for more. He'd rob her of her pride, then her father of his money. And by the time he left this part of the country, he'd have a roll of money big enough to choke a horse.

NINETEEN

Jackson spent a week riding the nearby eastern slopes of the Big Horn Mountains, but it took him only two days to spot the bay stallion and his large band of mares.

The stallion really was quite magnificent, with a blaze on its face, two white stockings, and powerful front- and hindquarters. But unfortunately, the stallion did not appear to be a young horse, and Jackson had the instant impression that the animal, even if gelded and broken, could never be completely trusted. There was just a point in time when a stallion crossed over the line and became so wild that nothing man could do would ever tame its spirit. Some mustangers thought that if a stallion were gelded and broken by age five, it could be redeemed as a saddle horse. Jackson thought the age was more like two or three.

"Hell," he muttered to himself as he watched the powerful horse mount one of his mares and vigorously implant his seed deep into her thick body, "if I had that many mares to service and someone cut off my balls, I don't guess I would ever regard them as a friend either."

For two more days, Jackson studied the comings and

goings of the mustangs, and when he was sure that he understood their daily patterns, he rode back down to the Pierce ranch.

"Mr. Pierce," he said, standing in the old rancher's living room, "I can catch that stallion and his mares, but I'll need some help."

"How much help?"

"Five cowboys."

"I don't know," Pierce said. "I'm a little shorthanded now anyway."

"You either give me the men, or that stallion will keep stealing your good saddle mares."

"How do I know that you'll have any more luck than we've had already?"

"You don't. But since I'm not on your payroll, I guess you could assume that I'm also gambling my time."

"Your time might not be worth much," Carole interrupted, a mocking smile on her lips.

"That's up to you to find out," he said, lowering his eyes to her breasts until her cheeks began to grow pink with embarrassment.

Pierce looked sideways at his daughter. If he realized what Jackson had done to her, he did not let it show. "What do you think, Carole?"

"I think he's got some pretty big talk to back up."

"So do I," the old rancher said. "But I'm still inclined to give him the cowboys he needs."

"One thing I forgot to mention," Jackson said. "I pick 'em."

"Why?

Jackson looked at Carole, whose eyes were boring into him. "I just want to make damn sure that the men I take understand that I'm in charge and that they'll obey my orders and not someone else's."

Pierce scowled. "Now, wait just a minute here, Smith! What we are talking about are you using *my* cowboys, who will be mounted on *my* horses. Men that are on *my* payroll.

I think that means I should have some say in what goes on out there."

"Of course it does, Pa," Carole said. "And I ought to be the one that makes sure our own interests are protected."

Jackson could have kicked the little bitch for saying that, but now that it was out, he made the best of things.

"Listen, Mr. Pierce. Give me the cowboys I choose, and when this is all done, I'll divide up the herd with you. That means you'll get twenty or thirty good mares."

"Hell," Pierce snorted, "most of them are mine anyway!"

"Not if you can't capture them."

Pierce could see the logic in this. "If you turn out to be all talk, I'm going to turn some of the boys loose on you."

The old rancher looked at his daughter, and when she did not object, he said, "When do you want to get after them mustangs?"

"Day after tomorrow?"

"No catch pens or corrals to build?"

"No," Jackson said. "Two days ago I found a box canyon, and I cut and ragged a few logs, so I think we can drive the stallion into the canyon and close the trap before he figures out he's been tricked and tries to come back out."

"If he does, you got to shoot him," Pierce said, his old hands clenched into fists. "You get him, the mares will be easy. You let him get away, he'll keep right on stealin' from me the way he has for almost three years now."

"I want him alive if possible," Jackson said. "I want to ride him."

"Why?" Carole demanded. "You told me yourself that he would probably always be an outlaw. Why risk your neck on a horse that big and strong?"

Jackson shrugged. "I hadn't thought of it that way until now. And you're right, I did say that I thought that stallion was worthless as a potential saddle horse. But there's something in me that makes it important that I ride him."

"It doesn't make any sense," she said.

"No," Jackson was forced to agree, "except that Matheson

and a few of his friends have been goading me a little, and I'd just like to see their faces when I ride that stallion to a standstill after he gets piled in the dirt."

"Matheson is damned good," Pierce growled. "If he can't ride that outlaw, I doubt you can, either."

Carole nodded smugly. "My father is right. Ted rides like he had glue in his pants."

"First we'll catch the stallion," Jackson said with just the trace of a smile. "Then we'll see who can really ride the wild ones."

When he said "wild ones," Jackson looked right into Carole's eyes, and she knew that he was referring to her as well as the stallion, because she blushed deeply.

"Tomorrow morning," Jackson said, "we'll be leaving long before daylight."

"I'm coming, too," Carole said. "I can ride as well as most of our cowboys, and I can handle a rope."

Jackson would have preferred that Carole not come along. With her in attendance, the cowboys he chose might tend to defer to her instructions rather than his own. But he could see that old man Pierce was pleased that someone he could trust was going, and so Jackson decided not to make this point an issue.

"All right," he said, "but we're riding out of here long before sunrise. We've got to be in place before those mustangs come down to drink, and everyone has to know what the hell is expected."

"Just knock on my door when you wake up the others," Carole said. "And I'll be ready."

"I will," Jackson promised. "Count on it."

That evening after dinner, Jackson called aside the five men he decided to use and told them his plan. "I'll wake you up and we'll ride out at least three hours before sunrise."

Not surprisingly, the five cowboys he'd chosen were not very enthusiastic. One of them, a lad of about eighteen named Charley Pike, said, "Hell, we've been trying as long as I've ridden for this outfit to get that bay stallion, and we haven't even been able to get a rifle bullet in him."

"They'll be no rifles allowed on this roundup," Jackson said. "We either trap them, or they get away."

Upon overhearing this, Ted Matheson sneered, "Smith, not only won't you catch that stallion, you probably won't even see the sonofabitch."

Jackson felt his stomach tighten. "I'll not only catch him, but I'll bet you your own boots and saddle against my boots and saddle that you won't be able to ride him, but I'll do it to a standstill."

Matheson bristled. "All I've heard from you is a lot of big talk. You ain't showed me or anyone else on this ranch a damn thing."

Jackson leaned back against the bunk bed where his bedroll lay. "Just wait until tomorrow afternoon. After I catch those mustang mares, you'll have something to do around here again other than drool over Carole."

Matheson's face contorted with rage, and his hands balled at his sides. "You sonofabitch! I think I'm going to beat the living hell out of you."

Jackson pushed off from the bunks. He looked around the Spartan bunkhouse at the other cowboys. "It's just him and me, right?"

The cowboys exchanged glances, and when one nodded his head solemnly, they all nodded in agreement.

"Well then, come on!" Matheson raged, turning toward the open doorway.

As the bronc buster was moving outside, Jackson drove his boot up between the man's forked legs so hard he lifted the younger man completely off his feet. Matheson hollered with pain and pitched forward to land in the dirt outside.

Jackson started after him, but one of the cowboys, an older man named Ray, stepped in the way.

"Give him a minute," he said in clear warning.

"Sure," Jackson replied with a shrug to indicate he didn't much care.

The cowboys refused to meet Jackson's eyes, but they could hear Matheson groaning with pain as he pulled himself to his feet, hands cupping his crotch.

"He's on his feet," Jackson said.

"That's all he is," Ray growled. "Give him another minute."

Jackson curbed his anger. "You know, boys," he drawled, "Matheson has been after my ass since the moment I first showed up on this ranch. Up to now I've been letting him talk, but I guess that each and every one of us has our limits."

"You didn't need to kick him from behind that way," a cowboy snarled.

"Sure I did," Jackson said. "If a man challenges you, you got every right to do whatever it takes to win. I just gave myself a little edge. But each second that we wait, I'm losing it. So come on, Ray, step aside and let me and Ted settle this with our fists."

Ray craned his head around and saw that the Pierce ranch bronc buster was regaining a little of his color, though his eyes and the corners of his mouth were still pinched with pain.

"All right, Smith."

Jackson did not wait for a second invitation but went right after the younger, heavier man. His punch came so fast that Matheson was still cupping his crotch when he was knocked down with a smashing uppercut to the jaw.

"Get up!" Jackson ordered. "You wanted a fight, you got one."

Matheson was tough. Despite being dazed and in tremendous pain, he cursed and sprang to his feet, then charged with outstretched arms. Jackson jumped aside, locked his fists, and slammed them down against the base of Matheson's skull. The young bronc rider grunted and ate dirt. Before he could recover, Jackson buried the sharp toe of his boot in the man's side.

"Ahhh!" Matheson cried.

Jackson would have booted him again except that Ray grabbed and spun him around. "You sonofabitch, try me!"

Jackson wanted to and would have, except that Ray was popular, and beating him would have brought the whole crew down on him.

"It's over," Jackson said, reining in his fury.

"Goddamn you!" Matheson cried. "You broke my ribs!"

Jackson looked down at the kid. "Maybe next time you challenge a man, you'll remember that you're just a boy who wears a man's clothing."

Jackson pushed back inside the bunkhouse and undressed. He could not keep from smiling, and the blood that pounded through his veins made him feel twenty years old again. Goddamn, he thought, if I could stay off the whiskey and leave alone the bad women, I'd never grow old.

They brought Matheson back into the bunkhouse and stripped off his shirt, then his boots and pants.

"I think we'd better go tell Mr. Pierce that Ted has at least a couple of broken ribs," Ray said. "Could be he'll send for the doctor."

"No!" Matheson cried. "I don't want no doctor! Just bind me up and I'll be all right!"

"You sure?"

Matheson nodded, his face white with pain. "I'll be all right. My balls are hurting ten times worse than my ribs."

The cowboys glared in unison at Jackson, but he pretended not to notice as he pulled off his own pants and climbed up into his bunk.

"The five of you that are coming with me had better turn in early if you want any shut-eye tonight."

"You can go to hell!" one of the men swore.

Jackson chuckled to himself. "You don't have to like it, but you had damn sure better be ready when I come around in a few hours."

Ted Matheson cursed him in English and then in Spanish, but as Jackson lay down on his bunk and closed his eyes, he was thinking of Carole Pierce and how, once the other cowboys finally went to sleep, he might enjoy going to pay her a little wake-up visit around midnight.

Why not? he asked himself with a broad grin at the ceiling. She won't put up any more of a fight than her bronc buster.

TWENTY

Clint stood beside his horse and looked at his friends. "Well," he said a little awkwardly, "I never liked long good-byes, so I'll just say *adiós*."

Milly came to his side. She reached up and touched the heavy bandage still wrapped turbanlike around his head.

"The doctor says that if you try to gallop that big gelding of yours, it'll give you the worst kind of headache. He says it might even cause you to black out on the trail. You've got to promise you'll not hurry."

"I promise."

"And you'll promise not to kill my brother if there is any way to take him alive?"

"For about the tenth time," Clint said with more than a little exasperation, "I promise I won't shoot him on sight but will give him a chance to surrender."

"Thank you," Milly said, kissing his cheek and stepping back.

Ben Bandy extended his big hand, and when Clint shook it, it felt as if he were grabbing a hoof rasp. "You sure you don't need me to come along?"

"No," Clint said, "as long as you've checked my horse so he don't throw any more shoes."

"I have, and he's fine. Will you come visit me and the missus in Huggins?"

"If I'm ever that way, sure."

"We'd like to name our first son after you, Clint," Milly said proudly.

"We would?"

"Yes."

Ben's face darkened. "I didn't agree to that!"

"Well, I was going to ask you. I didn't think you'd mind."

Clint tried to intercede. "It's all right. I—"

But Ben cut him off. "Milly, I was hoping we'd name him after me."

"All right," Milly amended quickly, "our second son."

Ben relaxed, and that meant that Clint did as well. "Thank you, Milly. I'm flattered."

"Well," Ben said a little gruffly, "you just watch your back. That Jackson Lane isn't—"

"Ben! You don't need to be saying bad things about my brother."

"I was just trying to warn him."

"He's the Gunsmith," Milly said, looking into Clint's eyes, "and he knows all the tricks."

Babette came to the rescue before the newlyweds could get into a full-blown argument.

"Clint, you be careful with Jackson. He's good with a gun and he's smart when he's sober, cunning when he's drunk."

Clint took the dance-hall girl into his arms. He'd grown very attached to her during the time he'd been recovering, and he meant to come back and renew their acquaintance as soon as possible.

"You ought to quit the Yellow Bird Saloon for another line of work," he said, meaning it.

"So far I've never had a good reason to quit," she said coyly. "Are you giving me one?"

Clint gulped. "Well . . . uh . . ."

"That's what I thought," Babette said. "So why don't you just take care of yourself, and when this is all done, hurry on back to pay me a longer visit."

Babette patted him on the chest. "Honey, I want to see what you can do when you're completely healthy."

Clint felt his own cheeks warm as he climbed into the saddle and waved good-bye to them, then rode north.

Three days later, he finally got his first lead on Jackson Lane.

"Said his name was Jack Smith," a freighter just north of Cheyenne recalled. "Of course, everyone who don't want anyone to know their past always calls themself Smith. That's why there are so damn many of them."

"I see." Clint pulled his Stetson down. "Did you get any idea where he was going?"

The freighter shook his head, but then he snapped his fingers and said, "By damn, he did say something that stands out in my mind."

"What?"

"He said that he'd heard that there were a lot of fine mustangs just waiting to be captured up against the eastern slopes of the Big Horn Mountains."

Clint grinned. "Thanks."

"You going after mustangs, too?" the man asked.

"Nope. I'm going after that mustanger."

"He done something wrong?"

Clint had started to ride past, but now he reined his horse in. "You could say that. He shot me in the head and knocked his own sister through a second-story window. He even used a woman who loved and tried to protect him as a bullet shield."

The freighter whistled softly. "Jack Smith did all those things?"

"His real name is Jackson Lane, and, yes, he sure did."

"Well, I hope you catch him then," the freighter said, "and

you make sure that you give him a little dose of rope justice. Hear now?"

Clint smiled and rode on toward the distant mountains with more confidence than he'd had in many, many weeks.

Ten hours later and forty miles north, Jackson rolled out of his bunk and dressed in the dark. He had not gone to sleep, and he guessed it was just after midnight.

Pulling on his clothes, he tiptoed out the door, easing it shut behind him. The moon was full when he crossed the ranch yard, carrying his boots in his hands. He mounted the ranch house porch steps and went inside, then crossed the living room and walked silently down the hallway.

Carole's door was shut but it wasn't locked, and when he entered her room, he placed his boots down on the floor beside her bed, undressed, and waited until his manhood lifted like a flagpole before he climbed in beside her.

"Wake up honey," he said, "it's time to ride."

She was sleeping heavily, but when he pushed her legs apart and mounted roughly, she came awake clawing and spitting. Jackson didn't let her cry out but covered her mouth with his own and used her until she moaned and stopped struggling.

"I hate you," she whispered, her body betraying her words.

"It don't matter what you think about me," he said, taking his rough pleasure. "Just as long as you know how to satisfy me whenever I want to be satisfied."

"You don't give me any respect," she whimpered. "You don't even like me!"

"Not much," he panted. "But then, I don't even like myself."

"And you wouldn't marry me either, would you?"

He gripped her muscular little bottom. "Hell, I don't know. When your father dies, you get this ranch, don't you?"

"Yes, but I'd never marry you if that's what you're after."

Jackson laughed softly. "You put a little more effort into this and I just might decide to marry you."

Carole hugged him tighter, and when he had finally had his fill of her and rolled away, she hissed, "You're such a bastard!"

He looked at her in the moonlight that came pouring through her curtains. "Let's get up and get moving," he said. "Come daylight, we're going to catch us some mustangs."

"You still mean to ride the stallion?"

"I do. Not only ride him, but win Ted Matheson's boots and saddle."

Carole was silent for a moment. She understood that a cowboy without his boots and his saddle was out of business. Those two items were his pride.

"You shouldn't have made that bet," she said, knowing how badly it would humiliate Ted. It would be worse than any physical beating.

"Of course I should have," Jackson said. "They aren't much, but I'll suggest that the boys take up a collection and buy them back for Matheson."

"He'd never take them. It would be a matter of pride."

"Then the hell with him!" Jackson swore. "I'll take them down to Cheyenne and hock them at a pawnshop."

Carole swallowed and climbed out of bed, feeling used and depressed. But she no longer doubted that this demon could do about anything he put his mind to. And if he was man enough to catch the stallion and ride it to a standstill, she'd probably be fool enough to marry the sonofabitch.

TWENTY-ONE

Jackson appeared out of the darkness and moved silently among Carole Pierce and the five mounted cowboys.

"All right," he whispered, "each of you knows where to go and what to do. Don't anyone make a sound until I fire my gun and start the mustangs running up toward our box canyon. Understand?"

They understood. Jackson had repeatedly drilled them on what he expected them to do after they'd left the Pierce ranch.

"Then let's ride. Carole, you stay close to me."

She bridled at being ordered but was smart enough not to say a word. If Jackson succeeded in capturing the stallion and his mustangs, all would be forgiven. But if not, Carole sure didn't want to be the cause of his failure and her father's wrath.

So she followed Jackson in the moonlight, and when they had ridden a quarter of a mile and were in position, she saw him pull his six-gun and then nod to her in signal.

Suddenly Jackson drove his spurs into the flanks of his horse, and the animal shot forward. Carole saw muzzle flames erupt skyward from Jackson's Colt. She drew her own pistol, and as she raced forward, they both emptied their guns at the pale moon.

The stallion bugled a call of warning and then drove his mares away from the water. Carole saw Jackson whipping his horse desperately to cut off the mustangs and keep them moving toward the mouth of the box canyon, some two miles away. She did not see how Jackson managed to block off the stallion, but somehow he did. Even in the darkness with only his dim silhouette, she recognized a truly remarkable piece of broken-ground riding.

The other cowboys began to funnel in on the stampeding herd of mustangs, being careful not to push the many foals so hard they would break their wind and be worthless as saddle horses. The mountainside seemed to shake with the thunder of horses' hooves, and Carole felt a wild sense of excitement. Holstering her empty six-gun, she began to whoop and holler until her throat ached.

"Keep them moving straight!" she heard Jackson crying over and over. "Don't let them turn! Keep them running hard!"

And they did. Each of them understood that capturing the mustangs depended on pushing them so hard that they did not have time to reason or to seek avenues of escape up the small barrancas or arroyos, or into the thick trees that clotted the mountainsides.

Once, Carole felt her racing horse stumble, and she instinctively yanked up on her reins. Somehow the animal recovered and charged on, close on the heels of the slowest mustang mares and their panicked foals.

The sun burst over the eastern horizon to reveal the sweating mustangs clearly. Carole could hear their labored breathing, and a sorrel mare heavily in foal sounded as if it were going to die, it was breathing so hard.

Through the thick dust she saw Jackson racing almost neck and neck with the stallion. Her own blood quickened when she realized that the stallion was desperately attempting to veer away and escape the trap but that Jackson, a quirt in his fist, was lashing the beast across the face and the neck, driving it forward into the canyon.

"Yaaa-hooo!" Carole shouted at the top of her lungs, the scream tearing raggedly at her throat.

Now she could see the box canyon, but so could the stallion, and it made one last effort to break free. Carole saw its head snake out, and she heard Jackson cry out in pain as the bay's long yellow teeth bit into his thigh. Jackson lashed over and over at the stallion, cutting it viciously until the animal released him and then was swept up into the canyon.

"We've got them!" Carole shouted in triumph when the last pregnant mare lumbered into the canyon and the cowboys threw themselves from their winded horses to start barricading the entrance behind them. "We've got them all!"

Jackson tied his horse and dismounted. When he tried to take a step, his leg buckled, and Carole saw that his pants were torn and bloodied.

"You'd better let me have a look at that leg."

"Later," he gritted, hobbling around to help the cowboys and working until he was certain that escape was impossible.

By the time it was fully daylight, the mustangs had stopped racing up and down the canyon seeking a way to freedom. Now the bay stallion stood guard alone against the men while his mares and offspring moved restlessly along the canyon walls.

"All right," Jackson said, hobbling toward his horse, "I'm going to need the two best men with a rope among you."

"That would be Mace and Charlie," Carole said. "But what are you going to do?"

"Rope the stallion and bring him down," Jackson said in a terse voice.

"Can't it wait a little while?" she asked. "You can barely stand on that leg."

"There's no water in this canyon," Jackson said. "After the run we've just put these mustangs through, they won't last a full day in this heat without water." He shook his head. "No, I won't make them suffer an hour longer than necessary. We need to get that stallion thrown and then get him blindfolded and a foreleg tied up to his chest. Once we've done that, and caught up the foals, we'll be able to lead him back to the ranch. The mares will follow us right on down to the corrals."

Jackson shook out his lariat. Mace and Charlie, grim-faced, did the same. Jackson said, "I don't have to tell you boys that we've got to get at least two of our ropes on that stallion or he'll eat one of us alive."

The two cowboys nodded with understanding.

"Then let's get this over with," Jackson said, galloping up the canyon, his rope already swinging over his head.

Carole held her breath as the stallion reared up on his hind legs and issued a challenge. When Jackson came in on the stallion, the animal ducked its head, but Jackson held his throw until the head was raised again. Carole's heart lifted with admiration as Jackson's loop settled neatly over the bay's neck and clamped down tight. The stallion, feeling the choking rope at its throat, laid back its ears and charged Jackson and his horse.

"Get him!" Carole shouted as Mace and Charlie raced in from opposite sides, ropes singing over their heads.

Both men threw at nearly the same instant, and when Charlie missed, Carole's heart jumped up into her throat. Fortunately, however, Mace's aim was true, and when he dallied his rope and pulled his horse skidding back on its haunches, the stallion hit the end of the rope and crashed to the earth, fighting and squealing.

Charlie was off his horse in an instant and, coming in from the stallion's back side, pounced on the bay's neck, wrapped his coat around its head, and used his sleeves to tie the coat securely.

"We've got him!" Charlie shouted.

Jackson wasn't ready to celebrate yet. He dismounted, fell, picked himself up, and, with Charlie's help, used a shorter rope to bind the stallion's foreleg to its barrel.

"Now we've got him," Jackson said, jumping aside and using a piece of cord to make damn sure the blindfold didn't slip free.

The rest was pretty simple. They roped the foals and yearlings, and within two hours they were driving the captured mustangs out of the canyon and back toward the ranch.

Carole rode beside Jackson. His face was pale with suffering, and she knew that the stallion's bite must have hurt him terribly.

"You won't try to ride him until that leg is better, will you?"

"I'll ride him before sundown," Jackson gritted. "But first we'll give Matheson his chance."

"Can't you just wait?"

"No," Jackson said, "I can't. I can't rest or even eat until this is finished."

Carole recognized the hard resolution in his face and knew it would be pointless to argue. Jackson seemed unable to tear his eyes from the stallion, and she desperately wished he would at least look at her.

"You were wonderful," she breathed. "I never saw anyone do what you did this morning."

He glanced aside at her. "Thanks, darlin'. I told you I was the best. Just wait until you see me ride that big bastard to a standstill."

It was an hour before sundown when they finally got the stallion saddled and Jackson looked over to Ted Matheson. "All right, hotshot, let's see how a good a bronc buster you really are and who's going to ride out of here without any boots or a saddle."

"Now, listen, you two," the old rancher said, "I don't know what's going on between the both of you, but I don't want either of you hurt. I say the best thing to do is shoot that stallion and forget this nonsense about riding him. He's too damned old to change, just like I am."

Matheson, his ribs heavily bandaged, looked plenty happy to dispose of the stallion and forget the bet, but Jackson wasn't.

"No, sir," he argued. "Your bronc buster and I have a bet, and it's going to stand. One of us is going to ride that stallion and the other is going to eat crow and ride out of here with his tail tucked between his legs."

The old rancher bristled. "You seem to forget whose ranch this is, Smith!"

"No, sir, I'm not. But I told you what I wanted when I set out to capture these mustangs and you told me I could do it my way."

"You've captured them. It's finished."

"Not for me it isn't," Jackson said, his voice hard and uncompromising. He stared at the young bronc rider. "You chickenin' out, or what?"

Matheson's cheeks flamed with humiliation. "Hell, no, I ain't! I'll take first ride."

"You got it, boy."

Matheson, slightly bent at the waist and in obvious pain, screwed his Stetson down tight and marched across the corral, where the blindfolded stallion was being held by three men. He shoved his boot in the saddle, and everyone heard him grunt with pain when he swung his leg over the stallion.

"This is crazy!" Carole shouted. "He's got broken ribs and shouldn't be riding a rocking chair, much less that outlaw."

"Let him go!" Matheson shouted.

The three cowboys were more than glad to pull the slipknot that tied the stallion's foreleg to his underside as well as unloosen the blindfold. They turned and fled as the bay shivered like a wet dog.

For an instant the stallion just stood in one place, quivering, and then he squealed in rage and erupted skyward. He came down straight-legged, and Carole saw Ted's neck snap like it was on the end of a rope. She also saw the young bronc rider's body break in the middle and heard Ted cry out in pain as the stallion dragged its big head down between its hooves and bucked like a thing gone crazy.

On the second buck, blood began to pour from Ted's nose, and by the fifth buck he lost a stirrup and was grabbing for all the leather he could find.

The stallion, sensing victory, bucked even harder, and it sunfished high in the air. Carole saw the bronc buster lose his second stirrup, and she noted the terror on his young face as he was hurled from his saddle. He struck the top rail of the breaking corral, and a pole splintered.

Everyone shouted, and two men grabbed Ted before he dropped back into the corral. The stallion was after him, biting and squealing. It was a miracle that Ted had escaped with his life.

The stallion began to race around the corral, clearing all the cowboys off the top rail as if they were roosting pigeons startled into sudden flight.

"Jeezuz!" Someone swore. "He's a killer!"

Jackson smiled. "He's that, all right. Let's rope and blindfold him again. It's my turn."

"No!" Carole heard herself cry. "Shoot him!"

But Jackson was already grabbing his rope and shouting orders for other cowboys to do the same. Fifteen minutes later the stallion was again snubbed down to a thick post in the center of the breaking corral, and a dirty bandanna blinded its wild, rolling eyes.

"This is insane!" Carole shouted.

"No, it ain't," Jackson said, a strange, almost peaceful look on his face. "It's what I was born to do: ride outlaws."

He smiled and winked at her. "I don't want you to feel bad when I say this, but I'd rather ride that stallion to a standstill than I would you, Carole."

"You sonofabitch," she hissed, "I hope he stomps you in the dust!"

Jackson shook his head. "For me, that might be the best way I could go."

He hobbled across the corral, jammed the toe of his boot into the stirrup, and swung into the saddle with the grace and lightness of a young man. Tearing off his Stetson and raising it high overhead, he shouted, "Boys, turn him loose!"

In that moment, Carole felt her heart swell and miss a beat. She hated Jack Smith, but God, wasn't he all man!

The moment the stallion's foreleg was dropped and the blindfold pulled away, the three cowboys scattered like frightened quail. Once more the stallion trembled. His coat was streaked with mud, and flecks of white foam made him look like he'd walked through a snowstorm. His mouth was torn and bleeding, and his eyes were marbles, rolling crazily around in circles.

Jackson looked no less crazed. His thin lips were pulled back from his teeth in a death grin as he drove his spurs into the stallion's heaving flanks.

The bay went berserk. It jumped straight up in the air, came down stiff-legged, and then bucked with maniacal fury round and round the pen.

For a few terrible, unreal minutes, Carole felt as if her breath would not come and as if she were witnessing a struggle that went beyond even life or death. Man and beast fought each other with a demented purpose that she could only gape at and then shrink back from as the struggle filled all her senses.

She saw blood pouring from Jackson's nose, just as it had from Ted's. At the same time, spurs were ripping at flesh, and the stallion was grunting with agony. On and on the struggle went, neither combatant willing to concede defeat.

Finally the stallion seemed to lose a step. Its power began to bleed away, and Carole sensed that its bucking was not quite as hard, its grunts of pain deeper, more abject. Jackson must have felt the tide turning in his favor as well, because he spurred even harder, forcing the issue to its resolution.

And then the stallion did something no one could have predicted. It threw itself into the fence, cracking pine rails, and it twisted, crushing Jackson's legs between its weight and the corral.

Jackson screamed. The stallion swung around, catlike, charged the opposite wall of the corral, and, at the last instant, twisted so that its body struck the poles full force.

Jackson tried to pull his broken leg upward but failed. They all heard him scream a second time.

"Get a rifle!" the rancher shouted. "Shoot that horse!"

But it was too late. Carole cried out helplessly as the stallion reared up and threw itself over backward. Jackson, clinging to the saddle, never had a chance. The saddle horn buried itself in his chest.

A moment later, a Winchester barked three times, and the stallion, which had been stomping Jackson's lifeless body, crumpled lifelessly to the earth.

The Gunsmith heard the rifle shots and put Duke into a hard run toward a pillar of dust rising near a ranch house. He brought his horse to a sliding standstill and dismounted to stand by a broken pole corral and watch a pretty girl cry beside a dead stallion and what was left of Jackson Lane.

Clint glanced sideways toward a handsome young cowboy who was holding his side and whose face was badly torn and bleeding.

"What happened?" Clint asked quietly.

"He didn't ride him to a standstill like he bragged," the young man said. "But he was still the best bronc buster I ever seen in my life. Probably that ever lived."

"Everyone said he was the best they ever saw," Clint said, expelling a deep breath. "I wish I'd have seen him ride."

The cowboy wiped his bloody face with his sleeved forearm. "You a friend of his?"

"Of his sister."

"She send for him?"

The Gunsmith climbed back onto Duke and surveyed the tragic picture once more. "Yeah," he said to the cowboy, "she sent for him."

Clint reined Duke around and started to ride away, but the cowboy hobbled after him, clutching his broken ribs. "Say, maybe she wants to know about this. Shall we just bury him here, or what?"

Clint reined Duke up for a moment and gave the question the thought it deserved. "You bury him here. Bury him with that bay stallion and put on his marker that he was the best bronc buster of 'em all."

"With the stallion?"

Clint nodded, reached into his pocket and extracted a twenty-dollar gold piece, which he pitched to the confused young cowboy.

"*With* the stallion," he repeated before he touched spurs and galloped away.

Watch for

THE GODFATHER

125th novel in the exciting GUNSMITH series
from Jove

Coming in May!

America's new star of the classic western

GILES TIPPETTE

author of *Hard Rock, Jailbreak* and *Crossfire*
is back with his newest, most exciting novel yet

SIXKILLER

Springtime on the Half-Moon ranch has never been
so hard. On top of running the biggest spread in
Matagorda County, Justa Williams is about to become
a daddy. Which means he's got a lot more to fight for
when Sam Sixkiller comes to town. With his pack of
wild cutthroats slicing a swath of mayhem all the way
from Galveston, Sixkiller now has his ice-cold eyes
on Blessing—and word has it he intends to pick the
town clean.

Now, backed by men more skilled with branding irons
than rifles, the Williams clan must fight to defend
their dream—with their wits, their courage, and their
guns. . . .

Turn the page
for an exciting preview of
SIXKILLER
by Giles Tippette

Coming in May from Jove Books!

It was late afternoon when I got on my horse and rode the half mile from the house I'd built for Nora, my wife, up to the big ranch house my father and my two younger brothers still occupied. I had good news, the kind of news that does a body good, and I had taken the short run pretty fast. The two-year-old bay colt I'd been riding lately was kind of surprised when I hit him with the spurs, but he'd been lazing around the little horse trap behind my house and was grateful for the chance to stretch his legs and impress me with his speed. So we made it over the rolling plains of our ranch, the Half-Moon, in mighty good time.

I pulled up just at the front door of the big house, dropped the reins to the ground so that the colt would stand, and then made my way up on the big wooden porch, the rowels of my spurs making a *ching-ching* sound as I walked. I opened the big front door and let myself into the hall that led back to the main parts of the house.

I was Justa Williams and I was boss of all thirty-thousand deeded acres of the place. I had been so since it had come my duty on the weakening of our father, Howard, through two unforunate incidents. The first had been the early demise of our mother, which had taken it out of Howard. That had been when he'd sort of started preparing me to take over the load. I'd been a hard sixteen or a soft seventeen at the time. The next level had jumped up when he'd got nicked in the lungs by a stray bullet. After that I'd had the job of boss. The place was run with my two younger brothers, Ben and Norris.

It had been a hard job but having Howard around had made the job easier. Now I had some good news for him and I meant him to take it so. So when I went clumping back toward his bedroom that was just off the office I went to yelling, "Howard! Howard!"

He'd been lying back on his daybed, and he got up at my approach and come out leaning on his cane. He said, "What the thunder!"

I said, "Old man, sit down."

I went over and poured us out a good three fingers of whiskey. I didn't even bother to water his as I was supposed to do because my news was so big. He looked on with a good deal of pleasure as I poured out the drink. He wasn't even supposed to drink whiskey, but he'd put up such a fuss that the doctor had finally given in and allowed him one well-watered whiskey a day. But Howard claimed he never could count very well and that sometimes he got mixed up and that one drink turned into four. But, hell, I couldn't blame him. Sitting around all day like he was forced to was enough to make anybody crave a drink even if it was just for something to do.

But now he seen he was going to get the straight stuff and he got a mighty big gleam in his eye. He took the glass when I handed it to him and said, "What's the occasion? Tryin' to kill me off?"

"Hell no," I said. "But a man can't make a proper toast with watered whiskey."

"That's a fact," he said. "Now what the thunder are we toasting?"

I clinked my glass with his. I said, "If all goes well you are going to be a grandfather."

"Lord A'mighty!" he said.

We said, "Luck" as was our custom and then knocked them back.

Then he set his glass down and said, "Well, I'll just be damned." He got a satisfied look on his face that I didn't reckon was all due to the whiskey. He said, "Been long enough in coming."

I said, "Hell, the way you keep me busy with this ranch's business I'm surprised I've had the time."

"Pshaw!" he said.

We stood there, kind of enjoying the moment, and then I nodded at the whiskey bottle and said, "You keep on sneaking drinks, you ain't likely to be around for the occasion."

He reared up and said, "Here now! When did I raise you to talk like that?"

I gave him a small smile and said, "Somewhere along the line." Then I set my glass down and said, "Howard, I've got to get to work. I just reckoned you'd want the news."

He said, "Guess it will be a boy?"

I give him a sarcastic look. I said, "Sure, Howard, and I've gone into the gypsy business."

Then I turned out of the house and went to looking for our foreman, Harley. It was early spring in the year of 1898 and we were coming into a swift calf crop after an unusually mild winter. We were about to have calves dropping all over the place, and with the quality of our crossbred beef, we couldn't afford to lose a one.

On the way across the ranch yard my youngest brother, Ben, came riding up. He was on a little prancing chestnut that wouldn't stay still while he was trying to talk to me. I knew he was schooling the little filly, but I said, a little impatiently, "Ben, either ride on off and talk to me later or make that damn horse stand. I can't catch but every other word."

Ben said, mildly, "Hell, don't get agitated. I just wanted to give you a piece of news you might be interested in."

I said, "All right, what is this piece of news?"

"One of the hands drifting the Shorthorn herd got sent back to the barn to pick up some stuff for Harley. He said he seen Lew Vara heading this way."

I was standing up near his horse. The animal had been worked pretty hard, and you could take the horse smell right up your nose off him. I said, "Well, okay. So the sheriff is coming. What you reckon we ought to do, get him a cake baked?"

He give me one of his sardonic looks. Ben and I were so much alike it was awful to contemplate. Only difference between us was that I was a good deal wiser and less hot-headed and he was an even size smaller than me. He said, "I reckon he'd rather have whiskey."

I said, "I got some news for you but I ain't going to tell you now."

"What is it?"

I wasn't about to tell him he might be an uncle under such circumstances. I gave his horse a whack on the rump and said, as he went off, "Tell you this evening after work. Now get, and tell Ray Hays I want to see him later on."

He rode off, and I walked back to the ranch house thinking about Lew Vara. Lew, outside of my family, was about the best friend I'd ever had. We'd started off, however, in a kind of peculiar way to make friends. Some eight or nine years past Lew and I had had about the worst fistfight I'd ever been in. It occurred at Crook's Saloon and Cafe in Blessing, the closest town to our ranch, about seven miles away, of which we owned a good part. The fight took nearly a half an hour, and we'd both did our dead level best to beat the other to death. I won the fight, but unfairly. Lew had had me down on the saloon floor and was in the process of finishing me off when my groping hand found a beer mug. I smashed him over the head with it in a last-ditch effort to keep my own head on my shoulders. It sent Lew to the infirmary for quite a long stay; I'd fractured his skull. When he was partially recovered Lew sent word to me that as soon as he was able, he was coming to kill me.

But it never happened. When he was free from medical care Lew took off for the Oklahoma Territory, and I didn't hear another word from him for four years. Next time I saw him he came into that very same saloon. I was sitting at a back table when I saw him come through the door. I eased my right leg forward so as to clear my revolver for a quick draw from the holster. But Lew just came up, stuck out his hand in a friendly gesture, and said he wanted to let bygones be bygones. He offered to buy me a drink, but I had a bottle on the table so I just told him to get himself a glass and take advantage of my hospitality.

Which he did.

After that Lew became a friend of the family and was important in helping the Williams family in about three confrontations where his gun and his savvy did a good deal to turn the tide in our favor. After that we ran him against the incumbent sheriff who we'd come to dislike and no longer trust. Lew had been reluctant at first, but I'd told him that money couldn't buy poverty but it could damn well buy the sheriff's job in Matagorda County. As a result he got elected, and so far as I was concerned, he did an outstanding job of keeping the peace in his territory.

Which wasn't saying a great deal because most of the trouble he had to deal with, outside of helping us, was the occasional Saturday night drunk and the odd Main Street dogfight.

So I walked back to the main ranch house wondering what he wanted. But I also knew that if it was in my power to give, Lew could have it.

I was standing on the porch about five minutes later when he came riding up. I said, "You want to come inside or talk outside?"

He swung off his horse. He said, "Let's get inside."

"You want coffee?"

"I could stand it."

"This going to be serious?"

"Is to me."

"All right."

I led him through the house to the dining room, where we generally, as a family, sat around and talked things out. I said, looking at Lew, "Get started on it."

He wouldn't face me. "Wait until the coffee comes. We can talk then."

About then Buttercup came staggering in with a couple of cups of coffee. It didn't much make any difference about what time of day or night it was, Buttercup might or might not be staggering. He was an old hand of our father's who'd helped to develop the Half-Moon. In his day he'd been about the best horse breaker around, but time and tumbles had taken their toll. But Howard wasn't a man to forget past loyalties so he'd kept Buttercup on as a cook. His real name was Butterfield, but me and my brothers had called him Buttercup, a name he clearly despised, for as long as I could remember. He was easily the best shot with a long-range rifle I'd ever seen. He had an old .50-caliber Sharps buffalo rifle, and even with his old eyes and seemingly unsteady hands he was deadly anywhere up to five hundred yards. On more than one occasion I'd had the benefit of that seemingly ageless ability. Now he set the coffee down for us and give all the indications of making himself at home. I said, "Buttercup, go on back out in the kitchen. This is a private conversation."

I sat. I picked up my coffee cup and blew on it and then took a sip. I said, "Let me have it, Lew."

He looked plain miserable. He said, "Justa, you and your family have done me a world of good. So has the town and the county. I used to be the trash of the alley and y'all helped bring me back from nothing." He looked away. He said, "That's why this is so damn hard."

"What's so damned hard?"

But instead of answering straight out he said, "They is going to be people that don't understand. That's why I want you to have the straight of it."

I said, with a little heat, "Goddammit, Lew, if you don't tell me what's going on I'm going to stretch you out over that kitchen stove in yonder."

He'd been looking away, but now he brought his gaze back to me and said, "I've got to resign, Justa. As sheriff. And not only that, I got to quit this part of the country."

Thoughts of his past life in the Oklahoma Territory flashed through my mind, when he'd been thought an outlaw and later proved innocent. I thought maybe that old business had come up again and he was going to have to flee for his life and his freedom. I said as much.

He give me a look and then made a short bark that I reckoned he took for a laugh. He said, "Naw, you got it about as backwards as can be. It's got to do with my days in the Oklahoma Territory all right, but it ain't the law. Pretty much the opposite of it. It's the outlaw part that's coming to plague me."

It took some doing, but I finally got the whole story out of him. It seemed that the old gang he'd fallen in with in Oklahoma had got wind of his being the sheriff of Matagorda County. They thought that Lew was still the same young hellion and that they had them a bird nest on the ground, what with him being sheriff and all. They'd sent word that they'd be in town in a few days and they figured to "pick the place clean." And they expected Lew's help.

"How'd you get word?"

Lew said, "Right now they are raising hell in Galveston, but they sent the first robin of spring down to let me know to get the welcome mat rolled out. Some kid about eighteen or nineteen. Thinks he's tough."

"Where's he?"

Lew jerked his head in the general direction of Blessing. "I throwed him in jail."

I said, "You got me confused. How is you quitting going to help the situation? Looks like with no law it would be even worse."

He said, "If I ain't here maybe they won't come. I plan to send the robin back with the message I ain't the sheriff and ain't even in the country. Besides, there's plenty of good men in the county for the job that won't attract the riffraff I seem to have done." He looked down at his coffee as if he was ashamed.

I didn't know what to say for a minute. This didn't sound like the Lew Vara I knew. I understood he wasn't afraid and I understood he thought he was doing what he thought was the best for everyone concerned, but I didn't think he was thinking too straight. I said, "Lew, how many of them is there?"

He said, tiredly, "About eighteen all told. Counting the robin in the jail. But they be a bunch of rough hombres. This town ain't equipped to handle such. Not without a whole lot of folks gettin' hurt. And I won't have that. I figured on an argument from you, Justa, but I ain't going to make no battlefield out of this town. I know this bunch. Or kinds like them." Then he raised his head and give me a hard look. "So I don't want no argument out of you. I come out to tell you what was what because I care about what you might think of me. Don't make me no mind about nobody else but I wanted you to know."

I got up. I said, "Finish your coffee. I got to ride over to my house. I'll be back inside of half an hour. Then we'll go into town and look into this matter."

He said, "Dammit, Justa, I done told you I—"

"Yeah, I know what you told me. I also know it ain't really what you want to do. Now we ain't going to argue and I ain't going to try to tell you what to do, but I am going to ask you to let us look into the situation a little before you light a shuck and go tearing out of here. Now will you wait until I ride over to the house and tell Nora I'm going into town?"

He looked uncomfortable, but, after a moment, he nodded. "All right," he said. "But it ain't going to change my mind none."

I said, "Just go in and visit with Howard until I get back. He don't get much company and even as sorry as you are you're better than nothing."

That at least did make him smile a bit. He sipped at his coffee, and I took out the back door to where my horse was waiting.

Nora met me at the front door when I came into the house. She said, "Well, how did the soon-to-be grandpa take it?"

I said, "Howard? Like to have knocked the heels off his boots. I give him a straight shot of whiskey in celebration. He's so damned tickled I don't reckon he's settled down yet."

"What about the others?"

I said, kind of cautiously, "Well, wasn't nobody else around. Ben's out with the herd and Norris is in Blessing. Naturally Buttercup is drunk."

Meanwhile I was kind of edging my way back toward our bedroom. She followed me. I was at the point of strapping on my gunbelt when she came into the room. She said, "Why are you putting on that gun?"

It was my sidegun, a .42/40-caliber Colts revolver that I'd been carrying for several years. I had two of them, one that I wore and one that I carried in my saddlebags. The gun was a .40-caliber chambered weapon on a .42-caliber frame. The heavier frame gave it a nice feel in the hand with very little barrel deflection, and the .40-caliber slug was big enough to stop any thing you could hit solid. It had been good luck for me and the best proof of that was that I was alive.

I said, kind of looking away from her, "Well, I've got to go into town."

"Why do you need your gun to go into town?"

I said, "Hell, Nora, I never go into town without a gun. You know that."

"What are you going into town for?"

I said, "Norris has got some papers for me to sign."

"I thought Norris was already in town. What does he need you to sign anything for?"

I kind of blew up. I said, "Dammit, Nora, what is with all these questions? I've got business. Ain't that good enough for you?"

She give me a cool look. "Yes," she said. "I don't mess in your business. It's only when you try and lie to me. Justa, you are the worst liar in the world."

"All right," I said. "All right. Lew Vara has got some trouble. Nothing serious. I'm going to give him a hand. God knows he's helped us out enough." I could hear her maid, Juanita, banging around in the kitchen. I said, "Look, why don't you get Juanita to hitch up the buggy and you and her go up to the big house and fix us a supper. I'll be back before dark and we'll all eat together and celebrate. What about that?"

She looked at me for a long moment. I could see her thinking about all the possibilities. Finally she said, "Are you going to run a risk on the day I've told you you're going to be a father?"

"Hell no!" I said. "What do you think? I'm going in to use a little influence for Lew's sake. I ain't going to be running any risks."

She made a little motion with her hand. "Then why the gun?"

"Hell, Nora, I don't even ride out into the pasture without a gun. Will you quit plaguing me?"

It took a second, but then her smooth, young face calmed down. She said, "I'm sorry, honey. Go and help Lew if you can. Juanita and I will go up to the big house and I'll personally see to supper. You better be back."

I give her a good, loving kiss and then made my adieus, left the house, and mounted my horse and rode off.

But I rode off with a little guilt nagging at me. I swear, it is hell on a man to answer all the tugs he gets on his sleeve. He gets pulled first one way and then the other. A man damn near needs to be made out of India rubber to handle all of them. No, I wasn't riding into no danger that March day, but if we didn't do something about it, it wouldn't be long before I would be.

J.R. ROBERTS
THE
GUNSMITH

___	THE GUNSMITH #111: GRAND CANYON GOLD	0-515-10528-7/$2.95
___	THE GUNSMITH #112: GUNS DON'T ARGUE	0-515-10548-1/$2.95
___	THE GUNSMITH #113: ST. LOUIS SHOWDOWN	0-515-10572-4/$2.95
___	THE GUNSMITH #114: FRONTIER JUSTICE	0-515-10599-6/$2.95
___	THE GUNSMITH #115: GAME OF DEATH	0-515-10615-1/$3.50
___	THE GUNSMITH #116: THE OREGON STRANGLER	0-515-10651-8/$3.50
___	THE GUNSMITH #117: BLOOD BROTHERS	0-515-10671-2/$3.50
___	THE GUNSMITH #118: SCARLET FURY	0-515-10691-7/$3.50
___	THE GUNSMITH #119: ARIZONA AMBUSH	0-515-10710-7/$3.50
___	THE GUNSMITH #120: THE VENGEANCE TRAIL	0-515-10735-2/$3.50
___	THE GUNSMITH #121: THE DEADLY DERRINGER	0-515-10755-7/$3.50
___	THE GUNSMITH #122: THE STAGECOACH KILLERS	0-515-10792-1/$3.50
___	THE GUNSMITH #123: FIVE AGAINST DEATH	0-515-10810-3/$3.50
___	THE GUNSMITH #124: MUSTANG MAN	0-515-10834-0/$3.50
___	THE GUNSMITH #125: THE GODFATHER (May 1992)	0-515-10851-0/$3.50

For Visa, MasterCard and American Express
orders ($10 minimum) call: 1-800-631-8571

Check book(s). Fill out coupon. Send to:
BERKLEY PUBLISHING GROUP
390 Murray Hill Pkwy., Dept. B
East Rutherford, NJ 07073

NAME _____

ADDRESS _____

CITY _____

STATE_____ ZIP _____

PLEASE ALLOW 6 WEEKS FOR DELIVERY.
PRICES ARE SUBJECT TO CHANGE
WITHOUT NOTICE

POSTAGE AND HANDLING:
$1.50 for one book, 50¢ for each additional. Do not exceed $4.50.

BOOK TOTAL	$ ____
POSTAGE & HANDLING	$ ____
APPLICABLE SALES TAX (CA, NJ, NY, PA)	$ ____
TOTAL AMOUNT DUE	$ ____

PAYABLE IN US FUNDS.
(No cash orders accepted.)

206d

If you enjoyed this book, subscribe now and get...

TWO FREE

A $7.00 VALUE–

If you would like to read more of the very best, most exciting, adventurous, action-packed Westerns being published today, you'll want to subscribe to True Value's Western Home Subscription Service.

Each month the editors of True Value will select the 6 very best Westerns from America's leading publishers for special readers like you. You'll be able to preview these new titles as soon as they are published, *FREE* for ten days with no obligation!

TWO FREE BOOKS

When you subscribe, we'll send you your first month's shipment of the newest and best 6 Westerns for you to preview. With your first shipment, two of these books will be yours as our introductory gift to you absolutely *FREE* (a $7.00 value), regardless of what you decide to do. If you like them, as much as we think you will, keep all six books but pay for just 4 at the low subscriber rate of just $2.75 each. If you decide to return them, keep 2 of the titles as our gift. No obligation.

Special Subscriber Savings

When you become a True Value subscriber you'll save money several ways. First, all regular monthly selections will be billed at the low subscriber price of just $2.75 each. That's at least a savings of $4.50 each month below the publishers price. Second, there is never any shipping, handling or other hidden charges—*Free home delivery*. What's more there is no minimum number of books you must buy, you may return any selection for full credit and you can cancel your subscription at any time. A TRUE VALUE!